CONTROLLER'S
obsession

LISA OLIVER & JP SAYLE

Copyright

Controller's Obsession – Obsessions #2

Copyright © JP Sayle and Lisa Oliver, 2024

Cover Design by Sleepy Fox Studio Designs

First Edition August 2024

Dedication

Dedication – Lisa Oliver

Thank you all so much for enjoying yet another ride with JP and myself. Remember, Love Wins.

Hug the ones you love, my friends.

Dedication –JP Sayle

Life is a journey that should never be taken alone. If you haven't got your people, then dive into a book, you'll always find them there waiting for you.

Controller's Obsession

A demon who punishes evildoers. A fastidious goat. What could they possibly have in common? Well, duh—nothing. Except Fate has other ideas.

When his friend Dakata needs help, Merihem—the 'controller' for the demon and human realm—charges in head-first without thinking about the consequences. For his trouble, he's cast up to the human realm and forced to take over Dakata's business and his home, all the while figuring out how to get back into the good graces of the king.

When he meets a small excitable goat—his 'blissful one'—life really gets interesting.

Peni left his home and got himself a cleaning job, where his only sanctuary is in the basement. Until a very large, naked demon invades his place of work, claiming he and Peni are 'blissful ones'. Yeah right. Except now, his goat half is acting up, the real housekeeper is angry with him, and he's clueless how to make his giant invader understand that when one of them is tiny, size really does matter.

And then there's the trifling inconvenience of someone trying to hurt them.

If they can survive all that, then maybe—just maybe—the universe got it right after all.

Controller's Obsession is book two in the Obsession series, proving that meeting a blissful one can change even a 'love 'em and leave 'em' demon.

Contents

Chapter One

Merihem

King Asmodeus glanced at Merihem, and that one look said it all. Merihem was in the demon shit. The level was yet to be determined. He didn't have to wait long when Asmodeus said, "Your actions have no rational basis, Merihem."

Being forcibly taken to Dakata's family home so Asmodeus could confront his friend's action in the demon realm, which Merihem had aided and abetted, didn't seem like such a good idea now the demon king was furious with him, too.

"He came at my request," Dakata, his closest and best friend, defended. "They all did." Merihem didn't need to look at the others in the room to scent their fear. Dakata's family had all helped their brother seek out the dryad Wanda in the demon realm. It was the destruction and death that came afterwards that had pissed off the king.

"I'm well aware of who aided you, Dakata. And as this is a situation, not encountered in many eons, I will need to seek council." Asmodeus's gaze swept the room, landing on each individual. "That does not mean this is an end to this matter. There will be consequences, as no one has the authority to run amok in my realm *without my permission.*"

With that threat barely hitting the air, Asmodeus whisked them, as in himself and Merihem, back to his palace, leaving the others behind, likely quaking in their boots. Merihem barely gained his footing when the King sat on his throne silently.

Oh fuck, he's brooding. This was not good!

In all the years he'd been 'Controller', Merihem had never pissed off Asmodeus enough to gain a threat or reprimand.

Asmodeus held all of Merihem's attention as the King of Demons tapped his long claws against the arm of the chair, looking down his long, thin nose at Merihem. "Can you explain why I shouldn't cast you into purgatory for the part you played in the destruction of Dusken?" His tone was almost bored while he continued to tap his claws. Tap-tap-tap-tap-tap-tap...

Such a ploy did not fool Merihem. Others had let their guard down and found themselves flayed alive for their stupidity and Merihem tried to avoid such a state. He had been Controller in the demon realm and, subsequently, the human realm too, for long enough to know he was in serious trouble.

His position gave him a lot of power and prestige, something he'd enjoyed. That was what he'd used to aid Silas, Dakata's blissful one, to find Wanda, Silas's sister.

A prat in the demon realm had mouthed off about Dakata's situation and, in turn had left Dakata vulnerable to attack. A position Merihem held a lot of guilt for, as well as a weight of responsibility. So, he had not considered fully—before helping his friend—just how furious Dakata would be. Never having had a blissful one—not that Merihem wanted one—he'd misjudged the destruction and mayhem Dakata would cause in his rampage.

Stupid—he couldn't deny it.

Considering everything now, he chose his words carefully. "Your Highness, Dakata's stressful situation brought out my need to assist him, as I have done since childhood. I made an error in judgement by not coming to you first. I apologize. In my defense, Wanda had limited time with her life connected directly to that of her trees."

"What concern is that of ours?" Asmodeus asked, just the faintest hint of irritation as his fangs clicked together.

"Dakata explained that Silas is his blissful one. That connection is something we were taught to hold as sacred. That we should honor that above all else."

At least Merihem was hoping he'd remembered what they'd taught him in demon school correctly. He'd not heard of an actual case before Dakata. The problem was that he didn't need to see the skepticism from their ruler. He had heard it when Asmodeus stated to Dakata that he'd need to seek advice. He never did that—*ever*. Asmodeus was rattled by Dakata's blissful one and that didn't bode well for anyone in the demon realm.

The huge demon rose from the ornate chair that sat in the middle of a room that, though in the demon realm, looked more like a human's home, only more decadent. Walls adorned in deep purple velvet matched the plump leather seats of the same color. The only chair that wasn't purple was the gold and black ornate throne the king used. The

Persian rugs scattered over the black marble were older than Merihem.

He moved silently towards Merihem, his coal-black eyes held Merihem's as he towered over him by half a foot. He was by far the biggest in the demon realm. Clawed fingers ran over Merihem's cheek, down to his throat, the claws digging in, giving him a reminder of exactly who was in charge.

Merihem didn't breathe or dare to swallow as they stared at each other, both weighing up the situation. Only one was in control, and it wasn't him.

Asmodeus's eyes flashed red, and his lips rose in a sinister smile. His lips moved, and Gebre appeared in the room, Merihem's underling.

"Gebre, how far are you from completing your controller training?"

Merihem winced at the reality of being stripped of his role and responsibilities.

"Your Highness, if intensified, three or four days should see me ready."

He'd never be ready in Merihem's opinion because the other demon enjoyed some aspects of his role a little too much. Gebre relished the kill, prolonged it beyond what Merihem would class as necessary.

"Good." The claws drew blood as Merihem started to sweat about what was about to happen. The red ate up all of Asmodeus's eyes. "Finish his training, ex-Controller then you will find yourself banished to the human realm to help *your friend* until I find the answers I seek."

Four days later, that threat, the one that Merihem had hoped wouldn't happen, did. In Dakata's office, Merihem jabbed a finger into Dakata's massive chest, uncaring he was provoking his friend. "Asmodeus, he sent me here as a punishment for helping you without seeking permission. I'm stuck in this realm until,"—his fingers made a motion for inverted commas—"I prove I can be trusted." It stung. Asmodeus had been so fucking vague, it just added to the overall pissyness of the situation.

"Did he say how?" questioned Dakata, looking concerned.

"To keep your siblings in order!" Merihem grumbled, sagging as he said it. He glanced at Luka and Christa and groaned. "It's fucking babysitting. How damn degrading is that?"

"Can you put on some clothes?"

Merihem fired a warning look at Dakata. He hated wearing clothes; they scratched in unfortunate places. He waved a hand, and a second later, dressed in jeans and a T-shirt, he cursed his life. "I'll be fucking expected to wear clothes all the damn time because of others shitty sensibilities!"

"Unfortunately, yes, you will. Luka, Christa, and Scott might be okay with you being naked and in your demon form. Those you're going to need to work with closely won't be so understanding." Dakata's expression revealed sympathy, but it didn't fix what he said.

"You're expecting me to manage your business,"—he jabbed his meaty digit at Dakata's siblings, his blood pressure hiking up—"and these two as well!"

Dakata nodded. "Who better than our 'Controller'," he replied, looking far too smug for Merihem, who became tempted to knock his friend's—though that was a loose interpretation with how he was feeling right then—pristine teeth down his throat and see if Silas liked him then!

Merihem threw up his arms and got up to stomp about. Going with resignation—for the time being. He got in Scott's face, Dakata's personal assistant, who didn't so much as blink. "You're gonna have to use some sort of code with me because I ain't wearing clothes when I don't have to!"

"Thank you, Meri."

He glared at Dakata. "Don't thank me yet! And I want your house, as I'm gonna have to live somewhere."

An hour later, keys to the house dangling from his fingers, Merihem opened the door to the large townhouse. He could have done it the way he usually did, but he wasn't sure if he was supposed to use his demon powers or not. Asmodeus hadn't been very forthcoming with a do's and don'ts list, so he wasn't taking any chances.

Being the official babysitter to Dakata's squabbling siblings and in charge of a music business, he could probably do with his eyes closed. *I mean, how hard could it be?*

Merihem's thoughts were on how he could redeem himself and get the fuck out of dodge when something caught his attention. He paused, his large head tilting to one side as he listened.

Was someone strangling a cat?

"Hello?" he called out. He paused long enough for someone to reply, but getting nothing, he bent and slipped off his sneakers. Bare footed he strolled through the lower level checking rooms as he went.

The place was minimalist and a little too sterile for Merihem's tastes, but a cast out demon couldn't be too choosy. Following the noise—because in no realm could it be called singing—Merihem came to a halt in the kitchen's doorway.

His demon perked right up at the pert ass, swaying from side to side before giving a little shimmy as the dude scrubbing at the counter butchered the song that Merihem couldn't identify. Sound-canceling headphones explained why the guy continued to sing out of tune, unaware of his audience of one.

Amused despite his own pissed-off-ness, Merihem leaned on the doorframe, trying to recall if Dakata had mentioned he'd replaced his last cleaner. The woman of about fifty, who always scowled at Merihem when he was naked, was a definite contrast to the tiny cuteness in front of him. And okay, Merihem couldn't see his face, but he could do some damage to the ass in spraypainted-on jeans. It wasn't like he needed to see the hot ass's face when all he'd be doing was fucking that peach before he rolled off to fall asleep. Most people had the common sense to leave before he woke.

He clicked his fingers—this was definitely a time to use his powers—and his clothes disappeared just at the same time hot ass spun around. Somewhere in Merihem's mind, for the split second it registered, the powerful impact of their gazes locking, which was chased by a huge dose of unease.

The scream that ripped at the air was so loud it potentially burst Merihem's ear drums. Eyes of the palest blue widened with horror as they swept down Merihem's naked body.

Not quite the reaction he'd been hoping for!

Merihem's demon howled inside him. Before he could register what was happening, he was in his demon form—chasing a pygmy goat around the kitchen. "*Mine,*" his demon growled with grabby hands.

Merihem's insides felt like they'd become plaited together as he attempted to do something—anything to prevent his demon from grabbing hold of the goat. *Don't touch it.*

"*Mine.*"

I fucking heard you. But think about it…

Panic, it was kicking Merihem's ass, even with his demon giving chase.

The head of the goat—who'd somehow managed to evade them on the chase around the large center kitchen aisle—connected with the back of Merihem's lower calf with enough force that the shock had them tumbling over the size sixteen feet.

He landed on his back hard enough that his bones rattled. Winded, breathless, and at a total loss at how the tiniest white goat could send him toppling, Merihem wasn't prepared for the goat's next move.

A blur of white fur caught his attention when the goat spun on its little four legs between his and lifted its hind legs to aim its hoofs directly at their nuts.

What the fuck!

His hands came down right as the hoofs connected, and he howled as the goat bleated madly before it made a mad dash out of the kitchen.

Stunned, with aching balls, Merihem lay on the floor, staring at the ceiling, struggling to breathe.

Who the fuck has just kicked us in the balls?

Who?

His demon actually had the audacity to laugh. *You know who!*

Chapter Two

Peni

Overwhelm imminent.

Overwhelm imminent.

Shut down in five…

Cut that out, you silly beast. We can't afford to faint right now. Peni had no idea why his goat form tended to speak like a computer in an old science fiction movie sometimes—it might have had something to do with the amount of time Peni spent watching them—but they could not faint, not now.

He was running, his tiny hooves slipping and sliding over the tiles he'd polished just that morning, heading outside. Peni needed to think, he needed to make sure his heart wasn't going to burst out of his chest, and he needed somewhere private to do that.

You can't leave him. Go back. Go back.

Maybe it was all the cleaning fluids he'd been using. Peni had absolutely no idea why his animal half wanted to go back and face a demon that looked like he'd just stepped out of a scene from a horror story. The demon was worth looking at from a purely aesthetic standpoint, but... Peni ran around the back garden and huddled under the nearest bush, his ears twitching at every foreign sound.

Mate.

Gods, now his goat half was bleating like a lost lamb, and that was not a good look. *Please, just shush. Keep an ear out for that demon and let me think.*

Peni was aware his usually sweet little goat side was muttering, but he knew how to tune that out. He was more focused on how, in heaven's name, his day had gone so wrong.

The demon in the house wasn't the one who owned it. Peni knew that much. Dakata, who owned the house, was almost a celebrity. Everyone knew who he was with his fancy cars, pockets of money, and the bands he'd made so successful.

But then I'm not the cleaner who's supposed to be working in the house either. Which meant technically, Peni couldn't consider the new demon an interloper when he was pretty much the same thing. Mrs. Danials, the woman who did have the job cleaning Dakata's house, was in Florida. She had been for months. "Those rich bastards never notice the help," she'd said, rather crudely, in Peni's opinion, when she'd offered him the job.

"You just do what has to be done. Make sure it's between the hours of nine and four, Monday to Friday, and the demon won't even notice I'm gone. I promise. I'm paying twenty bucks an hour, and I pay weekly on a Friday."

Mrs. Danials had said more about how her sister was sick, and she was the only one who could look after her, and things like that. Peni knew that was all lies because he could scent it. But the twenty dollars an hour was true and a godsend to a homeless little goat. Peni always felt as if he was constantly struggling to stay one step ahead of the wolves in the world. When he found out the house had a disused basement, Peni thought he'd won the lottery.

It was the basement window Peni was staring at now. He could just make out the outline of the little bed he'd rigged up for himself.

I have to get my things. My jeans, they have to be ruined, and my headphones, they dropped on the floor. We could've broken them. I saved for almost a month to buy them.

Stop thinking about that. His goat was still miffed. *That man in there is our mate, and you kicked him in the balls.*

It was your hooves on his balls, not my feet. Peni didn't want to even think about that, but it seemed his goat had other ideas.

That was a silly accident. It happens. You know, if you went back in there, on your two feet, explained that our hooves just slipped, and offered to give them a rub and a few smoochy kisses to make them feel better...

Are you talking about me doing that to the demon's balls? Peni was shocked and a teeny tiny bit intrigued.

They've probably got my hoof prints on them. You should kiss them better, at the very least.

Peni shook his head and waggled his ears. He liked that he could do that in his goat form. *I don't understand why you head-butted him in the first place. If you hadn't knocked him over, then you wouldn't have accidentally kicked his balls.*

I want to sniff his delicious-looking horns. Weren't they pretty and so studly? Worthy of the biggest goat in existence, you have to admit that. It's not like I could reach them when he was standing up. I can jump, but not that high... well, not from a standing start.

Don't use the word studly. Peni shivered. *That's just creepy and weird.* His father used to tell stories about how he'd gotten trapped in his animal form and 'put out to stud' was how he called it. Forced to impregnate females, all because the non-paranormals at the time had a fascination with tiny farm animals.

Peni wasn't sure how much force had actually been involved because his father usually had at least three or four women on the go at the same time. It was one of the reasons Peni had been homeless when he took the cleaning job from Mrs. Danials. His dad used to think it was fun to have orgies in the house and didn't see why Peni couldn't join in. Peni could think of at least a dozen reasons why not and left.

But that was then, and this was now. *Do you think he'll go out again soon?* Peni could hear the demon rampaging through the house. It was a wonder someone didn't call the police for all the roaring going on. *I've still got the study to clean, and it has to be close to four by now. I was looking forward to putting my feet up tonight and starting a new book.*

You have to go in there and talk to him. He's our mate.

There was that word again.

Peni sighed, although when a goat did that, it was more like a huff. A huff with a bit of lip flutter because goats could definitely be cute. *Why do you keep calling him our mate?* With his animal side, it was best to ask than assume. His goat form was tiny, but he was a determined beastie.

Because he is.

There was an example of the stubbornness. No explanation, just stating the most life-changing thing Peni could ever experience ever, as a fact.

I thought demons didn't have mates. They don't believe in them.

They don't call them that, but they have to have them because that one is ours.

Cleaning fluids. His goat's attitude had to be from working with too many cleaning fluids. *Mate or not,* Peni couldn't even think about that right now, *there's a mushroom pasta waiting for us in our little chiller. It only needs five minutes in the microwave. And remember, I bought brownies for dessert. Plus, we have three new books from the library waiting for us. A perfect evening, in other words.*

You wouldn't be spending time with books or a mushroom pasta if you just went in to speak to our mate. Seriously, I want to see if I left hoof marks…

On his balls, I know. Peni was grateful he could have conversations with his animal half. Not all paranormals were blessed like he was, and Peni was aware of how lonely his existence would be without his other half. It's not like he had any friends. But he sometimes wondered who was in charge of their shared form. *Do you think I could sneak back in there and grab my stuff from the kitchen?*

Yes. Yes. Let's go back inside and get your stuff.

Hmm. His goat was too eager. *I'll go on two feet so I can pick my things up.* Peni decided he wouldn't put it past his goat side to deliberately run up to the demon and pull a fainting act.

It's called a swoon. You have to admit he's swoon-worthy. He is. He is.

Peni shifted and then immediately glanced around. Shifter or not, he hated being naked outdoors. Or indoors. Or anywhere, really. He saw too much of that when he'd lived at home. Tiptoeing across the lawn, he opened the window into the basement and slipped inside. It was a bit of a jump down, but Peni was used to it.

Now, to work out where the demon was. Unlike the modern interior of the house, the stairs up into the main house were proper old and made of rickety wood. It was one of the reasons Peni believed that made him safe down in the space he'd created for himself. Anyone bigger than a hundred pounds would likely snap the wooden boards as soon as they stepped on them.

Making sure to avoid the boards that creaked, even under his weight, Peni crept up to the door and put his ear against it. In Dakata's house, the door to the basement they'd hidden in another cupboard—a big one in the laundry that backed onto the kitchen. Perfect for Peni to sneak in and out of if the owner of the house came home unexpectedly. That had only happened the once, but Peni had been so grateful for his escape route.

He had to be careful stepping into the cupboard. He kept his bucket and mops in there, and they would make a noise if he knocked them over. Cupping his hands over his cock and balls, Peni leaned against the cupboard door. All he could hear was his heart pounding. *Now is not the time to faint.*

A door slamming made him jump. Except as he listened, Peni realized the demon had left the house. *That's my cue.*

Pushing open the cupboard door, Peni tiptoed in double time through the laundry and into the kitchen, so grateful to see his clothes in a heap on the floor. *And my headphones, yes!*

Grabbing up his things, Peni eyed the discarded cloth he'd been using to clean the counter. It wasn't in his nature to leave it there, so he quickly scooped that up, too, whisking a clean cloth from the drawer and folding it, putting it on the edge of the kitchen sink. He threw the dirty one in the washtub in the laundry on his way back to the basement.

"I did it," Peni whispered as he was finally behind the basement door again. He made his way carefully down the stairs, and then had a thought, and dashed back up the stairs and slid across the bolt. He didn't like the idea of being locked in anywhere, but at least he'd have some warning if anyone was trying to get down to the patch of the basement he called home.

"Pasta and books. Pasta and books." Peni liked to put on his small television that he'd got from a thrift shop in the evenings. He kept the sound low, especially if Dakata was home. But as his current demon problem had turned up when most people were at work, Peni didn't dare risk it. "Let's get this pasta cooked before he comes home."

You should talk to him.

He's not home, and Peni might have felt a bit smug. There was nothing his goat could expect him to do about that. With luck, by the time Dakata or that other big demon came back, Peni would be asleep, and in the morning, everything would be back to normal.

Please let everything go back to normal.

Chapter Three

Merihem

His mad tearing around the house had done nothing to calm his demon half, in fact, if anything, he was starting to stress the neighbors would call the cops and have him arrested. They still did that on earth, and Merihem did not want to be locked in a cage after everything else his day had brought him.

Calm the fuck down.

Find him.

He tried reasoning.

You'll scare the fuck out of the little goat. He's like a twentieth of our size. Can't you see this won't fix things?

Find our blissful one.

Don't start with that shit. Merihem cupped his balls, recalling the insult those tiny hooves had inflicted. *He kicked us in the nuts. That does not say blissful one to me.*

You said it, he's scared.

You were the one roaring 'mine' at him.

That they were now back in the kitchen, and he stood having this conversation, possibly looking like a moron, passed them both by.

Yes... well, he is. It was a shock.

A shock... it's a fucking catastrophe, is what it is.

Merihem forced his demon to recede when he was about to start another tirade. His head wasn't in any place to go another round. He had better control of his demon than his best friend Dakata, or so he thought. After what had happened—he wasn't sure what to call it—Merihem wasn't sure.

There was one question on his mind as he strode up to Dakata's bedroom, going in search of something to wear. He wasn't going to use his powers right then, not when Merihem didn't know when he'd need them more. He was clueless, trying to figure out if getting kicked in the balls equated to him actually touching his blissful one.

Was there a loophole for that sort of thing?

He opened Dakata's closet and groaned at the sight of all the suits. "Who the fuck needs…" he counted, "forty suits! Who?" He rifled through the shelves, looking for something, anything that wasn't a suit.

At the back, he found a pair of jeans and a sweater that looked unworn by a band that Dakata managed. Dressed, he went to retrieve his sneakers from where he'd left them in the hallway before the disaster.

In one of the downstairs drawers where Dakata kept a stash of cash, Merihem grabbed a wad. He shoved that into his pocket, along with the house keys, after he exited the front door, locking it up behind him.

On the street, his head crowded with thoughts about how fucked up his life was, Merihem hailed a cab without thought and got in the back… then stared at the driver when he asked, "Where to, mate?"

Dakata was who Merihem thought about visiting. Face it, the whole damn business was all his friend's fault. Well, his and Silas, Dakata's blissful one, but sitting in the cab, that didn't seem like a wise idea when Merihem was as pissed at them as he was at anyone else.

He couldn't go to the demon realm. Besides the obvious—him getting kicked out and losing his job—he didn't want anyone down there knowing he had a slight problem.

He's not a problem, he's our blissful one. Sitting here will not find him, come on, get your act together.

"Mate, ya okay?"

No, he fucking wasn't, and his demon was giving him a fucking headache that went with the throbbing going on in his balls. How was he supposed to sort his mess out when he literally had no one to talk to about anything? How?

Merihem stabbed a hand into his jeans, pulled out some dollars, and handed them over, mumbling, "Sorry for wasting your time," as he got out and stalked back to the house.

He heard the guy mutter something about crazies before the car drove off. Up the front steps, Merihem stared at the locked door and hesitated about going back inside. Instead, he turned and sank down onto the top step, staring forlornly at the empty street. Darkness fell swiftly while he moped and ignored the fact he was hungry.

He'd have become horrified by his behavior if he'd not had other, more important things to worry about. Like, how was he going to find out who the little pygmy goat was without raising suspicion? How could he find out if what had happened to his balls actually constituted a lifelong commitment to the hottie?

Don't forget that cute little butt with his horns on the back of our leg.

Shut up. Merihem didn't need the reminder that the goat had actually hit him twice. Two touches! Fuck.

Everyone that knew him got he was a 'love em and leave em' kind of demon. He'd lived by that motto for a very long time. Up to now, Merihem had never considered changing it, not for anyone.

He's not anyone, he's our blissful one.

Turn off the damn record. A part of him was only now arguing with his demon side for form. It was a thing they both liked to do.

Find a way to fix this, or the record will turn into a permanent fixture in your life.

The threat was genuine, and Merihem didn't need to be attuned to his demon side to know it. *Can't you be reasonable?*

Find him, and I'll show you exactly how reasonable I can be.

Merihem heaved a sigh and gave in. He got up off the step, wiping the dust off his ass to swing around, coming to a decision. Doing nothing, was it really an option?

No.

So where did that leave him?

Going to find our tiny goat and...

One step at a time, okay!

Whatever you say.

Merihem felt his demon's glee and satisfaction at having won the first round.

We have to find him first, so don't go getting excited.

We can use our power for that.

No, we can't! We don't want Asmodeus suspecting anything, we're already in his bad books.

Oh... bad books? What's that?

Merihem opened the door and tried to think of a way to explain it when something he'd not noticed when he'd first entered the house struck. The unfamiliar scent, one that gave a powerful punch to his balls that matched the hooves kicking him earlier.

Because of his demon being hell bent on finding the goat in his rampage, they'd not taken the time to scent the place. A mad dash through the house bellowing 'mine' at the top of his lungs wasn't rational. They needed to be rational about this.

Rational...

Yes, rational. We use our other senses, the ones that don't require using our power. Warming to the idea, inside, Merihem blocked his other half, his nose wrinkling as he sniffed the air. He followed the unfamiliar scent to where it was strongest.

He'd been coming to Dakata's house for a long time, and he knew how it smelled. Knew where everything was... he came to an abrupt halt in the kitchen and stared.

His eyes gleamed with the knowledge the tiny goat hadn't disappeared—or not far—when the clothes and head-phones were nowhere in sight. The cloth the little one had dropped was gone and on the side of the sink was a clean one. Merihem picked it up and sniffed. The goat's scent was all over it, and it was fresh.

He held on to the cloth and followed his nose into the laundry room. There, he looked at the one door, opening it silently, he stared at the mops, bucket, and other cleaning stuff. Was the scent strongest in there?

Filtering out the other scents of detergents and whatever else, Merihem kept the tiny goat's smell as his focus. He edged into the small space, getting half a foot in, and scowled. The space was far too cramped for someone of his size. His gaze narrowed on the back wall… *but not for someone who was small.*

Did Dakata say the place had a basement?

His heart doing a little pitter-patter thing, Merihem backed out and carefully closed the door too, but not all the way as he'd found it. A grin that Dakata would have recognized instantly as wicked appeared while Merihem considered how best to find out, if indeed, the little goat had used that way as his escape route, and if he was the new cleaner who would be back the next day.

His demon was quivering with excitement and that suggested to Merihem he was going to have to keep a tight rein on his demon side, or they'd be back chasing a tiny goat around the house.

Merihem was a hunter. He'd trained for many years to stalk his prey.

Not prey!

He didn't respond because arguing with his demon half had so far proved fruitless and increased the risk of worsening the head pounding. No, Merihem had to think clearly if he was going to catch the little goat.

He placed the cloth back where he'd found it and left the kitchen, going upstairs to get as far away from where the goat's scent was strongest. He didn't need to have that playing havoc with his thoughts when he needed to be sensible. Shutting himself in the bedroom for good measure, he reached for the phone at the side of Dakata's bed. He dialed the number he knew by heart and waited as it rang.

Putting his thoughts in order, Merihem needed to clarify a few things first to give him a starting point and that he could do without raising suspicion. He was positive about it!

"What now?" Dakata growled breathlessly. "You've barely been in charge five minutes. You can't have fucked anything up already."

"Did I interrupt something?" Merihem asked sweetly and with a huge dollop of sarcasm, recalling he remained pissed at his friend for his situation and the current clus-terfuck that ensued.

Dakata grunted, and Merihem was sure he heard Silas moan in the background.

Oh, to the demon gods, were they…

"Fuck off, Meri… oh like that…" The next moan was all Dakata before he asked, "What do you want?"

Seeing as the situation could get out of hand quickly and with his current situation, Merihem didn't need any of Dakata's and Silas's sexual antics, giving him even bluer balls. "What times and days does your cleaner come in?"

"Huh… yeah…"

"Focus, Dakata," he snapped, his hand clenching tightly around the phone.

"Erm… Monday through Friday… while I'm at work… I…"

"Does she have an assistant?" he interrupted at the next round of groaning.

"Right there…" he whimpered down Merihem's ear. "No… what assistant?"

"Great. Thanks." Merihem hung up and stared at the empty and spotless bedroom, his smile returning.

So, no assistant, then who was the guy?

His smile dimmed when thoughts of pulling the records of every employee that Dakata had went sailing out the window.

He plonked his ass down on the bed, deep frown lines appearing, then disappearing, as he mulled over his next step.

Spying…

Yep, that would totally work. *If the guy came back.*

Chapter Four

Peni

It was ten to nine the next day... roughly. Dakata had a large clock in his study that chimed every quarter hour, and if Peni strained his ears, he could hear it. Peni hadn't got as much sleep as he'd like. Between his goat bleating what felt like every five minutes about wanting their mate and him straining his ears every few minutes, wondering what the demon upstairs was doing—or more specifically, *which* demon was upstairs—Peni had been awake from the moment the sun rose.

His basement spot had one significant advantage—someone had insulated the floor with some kind of heating for the levels above. It meant if Peni was cautious, he could move around and have his television on, without being heard by the people in the main house.

Dakata, if he was home overnight, was usually gone by eight in the morning, even earlier most days. His workaholic habits gave Peni a chance to have a quick shower in the tiny cubicle someone had put in the basement and then forgotten. It wasn't tiled, only lined with plastic, but it had hot and cold running taps, and between that and the singular toilet and tiny hand sink, which sat next to the shower cubicle, it was enough for Peni. He'd always been cautious, never flushing the toilet until Dakata left for work, in case the pipes made a noise through the house. It's not like he could be in two places at once and check for that sort of thing.

You should've gone up and made him breakfast before he went out. Show our mate we can be useful for more than just cleaning. His goat piped up again as Peni poured himself a bowl of cereal, adding a splash of milk that he stored in his cooler. Going over to his small mass of cushions that made up his bed and chair all in one, he sat down quietly and dug his spoon into the bowl.

A huge demon like that needs a good start to his day.

Great. Now his goat was offering tips on demon nutrition. *Dakata doesn't eat breakfast. He barely eats here at all.* Yes, Peni was being deliberately obtuse, but he desperately wanted his day to be a normal one. Shower. Eat. Go upstairs and clean. His pay would be in his account once he got done for the day. Peni could go and buy a few bits of groceries and replenish his soap and shampoo before curling up for another quiet evening with his library books.

Dakata didn't come home last night. Our mate was the one who slept here last night.

Peni stilled in the act of putting another spoonful of cereal in his mouth, his eyes darting around his space. *How do you know that? It's not like we can hear anyone moving much around the floors above.*

Our demon slams the doors differently to Dakata. Dakata's are short and sharp, as if he's not thinking about it. Our demon does it deliberately. Bedroom door. Closet door. Bathroom door. Front door. I think he knows we're here, and he's sending us a message. Isn't that sweet of him?

No! Peni didn't even want to consider that possibility. The demon with the big balls couldn't know he was staying in the basement. *He can't find us here. I'd get fired if he knew we were down here... and Mrs. Danials would get into trouble... Don't you see? We'd be homeless again.*

Our demon wouldn't let us be homeless.

Yep, you keep telling yourself that, but Peni kept that message to himself. Just the stress of being put out, of having nowhere to go, was enough to give him a headache. He'd spent more time than he'd like to think about sleeping rough. The world wasn't kind to little shifters like him.

It's time to go upstairs and start work. His darn goat was almost singing he was so happy about it. But Peni knew that was what he had to do—it was what he would normally do. The front door had slammed shut just before eight. He'd showered, wiping down the plastic so it was as clean as the day whoever had installed it, and he'd eaten. Peni couldn't put it off anymore.

Rinsing his bowl in the tiny sink, Peni left it in there to drain, rubbing his hands dry on a small towel he kept handy for that sort of thing. He gathered up his change of clothes. It was laundry day, and Dakata never seemed to notice when he washed his clothes in with the used linen in the house. His headphones he looked at and left behind. Peni wanted to keep his wits about him. There would be no singing for him while he was so nervous—which was a shame because Peni loved to sing... as long as no one was listening to him.

Everything's normal. The demon is at work. The house is mine for the next seven hours. Keeping that thought forefront in his mind, Peni crept upstairs, wincing as the bolt he'd latched the night before squeaked on opening. He made a mental note to oil that later. The door opened quietly enough, but Peni paused as he saw the outer cupboard door was open. *I know I closed that when I came through it last night.*

Just the idea that the demon could be lurking on the other side of the door, waiting to jump out and grab him, had Peni thinking about spending the day in the basement. But if he did that, then Peni knew he would have to spend that day moving out. He justified he wasn't doing anything wrong by staying downstairs because he cleaned the entire house methodically from top to bottom. And Peni worked hard so he didn't feel he was doing anything wrong... even though he knew technically he was.

No. Peni was determined he was going to have a normal day. It was highly possible the demon spilled something on the floor and needed the mop to wipe it up. Peni ignored the fact that the mop head was dry and moved through the cupboard, pushing the door open wide and peering around both edges.

No demon. *He's gone to work. Stop being silly.* Peni stepped out and went over to the huge industrial washing machine Dakata had. *Time to change the linens, get the machines going, and then I'll clean the study and the up-stairs bedrooms. Just another normal day.*

We are not rolling all over Dakata's bed. What is wrong with you? Peni was hanging on by his last nerve. The first couple of hours had been normal enough. He got his clothes washed and dried quickly enough while he was cleaning the study, which was the one thing he hadn't finished the day before. There was just a coffee mug left in the kitchen, so Peni washed that and put it away before setting up the coffee machine for a fresh brew for when Dakata came home.

Dakata, not the other demon. In fact, Peni had decided by the time he made his way upstairs that the demon who'd chased him around the kitchen the day before was clearly just a random overnight visitor. Probably some poor demon who Dakata had let stay because he was busy doing something else. Nothing to worry about, in other words.

His goat half had great fun snorting at that idea. *A mate will not leave us.* Something else Peni ignored. By all that was holy, the moment he went into the main bedroom, his goat started acting as though he was drunk.

Roll on it. Smother our scent all over his covers. He'll love it, and it'll make him feel spicy.

We're not a cat shifter. Goats do not leave scents for others to find. Peni definitely didn't want a "spicy" demon running about the house. He took the cover off the bed and reached for the sheets when, all of a sudden, his knees went weak. "What's happening?" Stunned, Peni spoke out loud.

You have to. Do it.

Right. So his goat was trying to force Peni to do something he would absolutely never do. "Cleaners do not roll on their employer's bed. That is undignified and a tremendous breach of trust. It's wrong." He gathered up the sheets into a large roll to take downstairs when he got a prickly feeling across the back of his neck. The feeling a prey animal would get when a predator was nearby.

What are you doing to me now?

His arms filled with the dirty linen, Peni looked around for somewhere to hide, just in case. *Who's here?*

No one. We're the only ones in the house.

Rubbing the back of his neck, Peni wasn't so sure, but he hadn't heard the front door, and he had been listening out for it. Giving himself a determined shake, he took the dirty sheets down to the washing machine and grabbed fresh sheets and towels from the linen cupboard.

The prickly feeling came back as he went back upstairs. *Are you sure someone's not watching us?*

There's no one here but us.

I'm going out of my mind, another thought Peni kept to himself because his goat was not being helpful. Inside, he knew he was one loud noise away from running out of the house and never returning. He hurried to remake the bed with fresh sheets, taking the time to smooth out the wrinkles. Mrs. Danials had told him wrinkles were something Dakata absolutely wouldn't tolerate. The bed hadn't been made so crisply or quickly ever before.

Hurrying through to the bathroom, Peni got hit with another wobble in his knees. *Please stop doing that,* he begged his animal half as he quickly bundled up three damp towels that were hanging over the railing and replaced them with clean ones. Using the end of one of the drier used towels, he buffed a shine back into the taps on the basin, checking the shower door. It wasn't too bad, and with Peni worried he was going to collapse on the floor in a heap any minute, he decided to leave that for another day.

No, don't leave the bathroom. Our demon's scent is so delicious in there. Can't you imagine him standing there all naked and dripping with water, just waiting for you to dry him off with your tongue?

Where do you get your weird ideas? Not from me, that's for sure. Peni almost fell, he was in such a rush to get down the stairs. That feeling of being watched hadn't eased. Peni's heart was racing, and he could hear the blood rush in his ears.

Wash the towels.

Dust the surfaces in the bedroom.

Vacuum the floors.

Peni kept working, but he'd never moved so fast in his life—that feeling of being watched persisting. By the time the vacuum was put away and the last of the linen was dried, folded, and put back in the linen cupboard, he felt as though he had run a marathon.

It was only three o'clock when Peni went back down to the basement, and out through the basement window, taking care to leave the latch ajar so he could get back in. He peered around the side of the house, making sure there were no cars around, before scuttling down the path and onto the street.

"I'll do some shopping. Maybe grab a takeaway for dinner. This is just my nerves rattling. Everything will be fine. It will be fine." But Peni couldn't shake that same feeling of being watched even as he left the house behind.

Do you think our demon likes pizza?

Peni groaned out loud. Unfortunately, he'd never found a way to silence the other half of his soul.

Chapter Five

Merihem

I knew it!

His eyes narrowed on the gorgeous creature who'd just walked into the kitchen, totally unaware he was being spied on.

Merihem had been really careful to act as Dakata would. He'd slept better than he'd expected in Dakata's bed, knowing the goat was down in the basement.

His demon half was actually okay with the plan he'd come up with that morning as he'd showered. So he'd allowed Merihem to vacate the house just in case the little one was watching him and Merihem hadn't figured out how. The little guy had managed not to be spotted by Dakata, so that said a lot about how evasive he could be.

Going to the office, yep, that was a necessary step, too, because he didn't want one of Dakata's brothers or his sister Christa landing on his doorstep and eliminating the possibility of a meeting. Merihem managed to focus long enough to deal with a few things at the office and had got Dakata's secretary, Scott, to keep him updated on anything important.

Then he'd got the taxicab to drop him a block from the house, and he'd started stalking his prey.

How many times do I have to say it? He's our blissful one!

Does it make a difference? Merihem argued back for form alone when, after peeking through the kitchen window around the back of the house, his heart tripped in his chest. Except Merihem wasn't stupid enough to go into the house. He'd decided to eliminate the possibility of his demon doing a repeat of the day before and chose to spy on the wee goat from outside the house.

He used his power to cloak himself, going with a spell rather than a flick of his fingers. A spell wouldn't alert his boss to what he was doing in the human realm. Merihem was a great climber, and he'd already assessed how to scale the outside of the house.

He'd caught sight of the bubble-butt disappearing out the kitchen door, and followed. He could see into Dakata's bedroom and waited.

When the little guy's head swiveled about better than any owl shifter, Merihem actually ducked before he realized he couldn't be seen.

A big problem was that other parts of him were vying for attention. Merihem's lower body reacted rather violently when the bubble butt faced him as their blissful one bent over the bed, his ass swaying as he tugged off sheets minutes later.

Merihem groaned under his breath. He hated to say it, but his demon half was right. Because the situation in his boxers comprised of his cock sword fighting with his underwear, trying to rip them apart to get what it wanted had never happened before.

The goat disappeared again, and Merihem took his time following him around, which would have been fun, if not for the situation in his pants that made contact with the brick walls. Cock versus brick wasn't fun!

By the time they were back in the kitchen, and everything looked to be clean and tidy, Merihem was ready to call mercy. He debated outside what his next move should be when he realized the guy had never reappeared from his cubbyhole.

A noise behind him had Merihem freezing in place when a window opened and out crawled the gorgeous guy. His delicious smell enticed Merihem to do something silly, or wicked, or both. The man went to take a step, only to come to a halt, looking back, directly at him.

The solid punch to the throat, chest, and cock, all together, was enough to render Merihem immobile, giving the little goat time to dart off.

His demon side got him moving, as Merihem hissed, *don't you even think about alerting him to our presence in the street!*

As if I'd be that stupid.

Right, like you weren't the one shouting 'mine' at the top of your lungs yesterday?

I was declaring our feelings, that's all.

Yeah, to the whole damn city. You're as bad as Dakata's demon.

The scowl he could feel when his demon did a stompy thing in his head, threatened to give him a headache again. *Listen, I can always go back to the house.* Merihem had no such intention. He wanted to figure out what his little goat was up to. It was the only way to size up the situation properly. Merihem wasn't a demon who rushed blindly into any situation, despite his demon's intentions.

Their little goat went into the bank, then came out two minutes later with a small bulge in his front jeans pocket.

So, he got paid at the bank, but by who? Merihem made a note of the bank. He could get Scott to see if they transferred the staff's wages into that particular branch.

Fascinated, Merihem watched the goat buy food, not a lot, but enough to fill a small brown sack. He treated himself to a small green-looking smoothie before he trotted off to the library. This was the only place where he took his time, going straight for the romance section. Merihem smirked when he picked up a book that was clearly about demons.

Grinning, he couldn't ever remember a time when he'd enjoyed spying on someone so much before.

His belly growled when the little goat finally stopped at a pizza place and grabbed four large slices of pie that had nothing on it but... vegetables.

Yuck. Where was the meat?

The scent of the melted cheese, which Merihem was partial to, did not compete with his blissful one's fragrance. So, by the time they got back to the house and the little bubble butt disappeared back through the window, Merihem was in a bit of a pickle.

He had to have strong words with himself as that delectable ass wiggled at him before disappearing.

Don't do anything rash!

Don't do anything rash.

If he kept saying it, surely it would sink in?

Move away from the window. You are far too big to try and squeeze through there.

Did the talking to he'd given himself help?

Did it fuck.

Merihem's hands balled, and he willed himself—not his demon, he hastened to add—to behave. He didn't breathe easy until he rounded the house, out of sight of the window, and plonked himself down on the steps like he'd done the day before.

He clicked his fingers to remove the spell and thumped at his cock for good measure, willing the thing to deflate.

He played over several awful situations he'd dealt with in the past that were gory enough to turn a demon's stomach and breathed in some fresh air.

How long he sat like that he'd no clue, but when his cock finally got with the program, Merihem stood up and unlocked the front door. One step inside, and he groaned anew, his body ramping the fuck back up at the intoxicating smell. *All that thumping and deep breathing was for nothing.*

His demon actually laughed at his predicament. *Go on, try to resist our blissful one.*

Sheer willpower had Merihem walk through the house and up the stairs to Dakata's bedroom. He didn't take one breath until he turned on the shower and twisted the dial until it couldn't get any colder before stripping and diving right in.

"Motherfucker," he cried out at the icy water blasting his cock and balls. Shards of glass, it felt like were trying to stab him.

He jumped right back out, water flicking over the clean surfaces, scowling. He hated cold showers. Demons were hot-blooded creatures by nature. He'd clearly lost all reason.

He's right downstairs, just go, knock on his door and ask him on a date.

"Are you for fucking real?" he exclaimed loudly, forgetting himself. "A date! I've never taken anyone on a date in my life."

Exactly. This is special. We have a blissful one, and we need to court him.

You've changed your tune.

Didn't you see how pretty he is, and how careful he was in taking care of the house for us? How he got romance books about us? He wants to be courted, not fucked.

This whole situation was getting out of hand, because now his demon side was actually making sense. To the demon gods, how?

Merihem twisted the tap around to hot and climbed back into the shower in a complete grump. His gurgling stomach reminded him he'd not eaten. He ignored his boner and washed and dried himself as quickly as possible.

He found some lounge pants that fit, if he ignored the obvious tenting, and went down to the kitchen to hunt up food.

He stopped at the counter, and a fucking huge smile spread over his face at the pizza box with a sticky note on it.

I bought some pizza and thought I'd share it.

No signature. No name. But that didn't matter as Merihem took the note and folded it like it was the most precious thing in the world. He eyed the three pieces of vegetarian pizza, his smile not dimming at all as he reached in, felt it was still warm, and ate a slice standing at the counter. Had that cute little bubble-butt re-heated his slices so it would be hot for him coming home from work?

His chest warmed at the very thought. Merihem's gaze roamed to the door, and he decided to stop fooling himself. One afternoon following his blissful one and he was... *smitten.*

To the demon lords, never utter that word again.

It's true, though you are.

Fuck all the way off back to hell, okay!

Don't be silly. So where are we taking him on our first-ever date? Movies? A restaurant? A museum? Oh, I know, what about a petting zoo?

Merihem rolled his eyes at the ceiling, inhaling the second piece of pizza. *I've no damn clue.*

But the first hurdle was asking the little goat to go out with him. How the hell did he do that?

Chapter Six

Peni

The pizza was gone from the kitchen counter the next morning. It was the weekend, a Saturday, but the demon still left the house just before eight in the morning, much like Dakata used to do. Actually, Dakata was rarely at the house all weekend, but Peni couldn't guarantee this other demon would do the same. Peni tried to resist, but curiosity had bitten him on the ass, and after going through his normal morning routine, he'd crept up into the house to check and see.

He liked it. His goat was hopping around on all four legs in Peni's head. *He liked it. He took our food and ate it.*

He could've just thrown it out. Peni went over to the trash, but all that was there was the empty box. *All right. He ate it. But he's a demon. He'd probably eat anything.*

You should've got meat on it. I mean, we did the cheese thing, but maybe next time…

Peni slapped the middle of his forehead. "Just stop," he said out loud. "We're not cooking for him. We don't need to buy food for him. The demon has more money than we'll ever see in our lives. One nice gesture, because you wouldn't let me eat my slices in peace. One gesture where I left him *three of my four slices* of pizza—pizza we could've been having for lunch and dinner today, and now I have to make do with a sandwich. By the horned ones, you will have me shifted and nibbling on the bushes in the garden at this rate when we're feeding a demon who can afford to buy any food he wants."

There was a moment's silence in his head. Peni went into the laundry and grabbed his cleaning rags and the bathroom spray. He really hadn't given that shower in the master bathroom a decent going over the day before. He was

almost at the top of the stairs when his goat said, *So...
what sort of garden plants are we talking about here? I
mean, the demon doesn't have anything juicy, like black-
berries in their garden, and the sunflowers are out of sea-
son this time of year. I suppose I could make do with some
of the foliage I've seen, but the pickings are slim. But you
could take me out to...*

Are you serious? Peni couldn't believe what he was hearing. *You'd rather give the demon all our food and have me
live on grass and weeds?*

Not grass. Peni could literally see his goat shaking his
head. *We don't eat grass. Only goats who can't find anything else will eat that stuff, and our demon's grass is covered in all sorts of chemicals. Ugh. You need to tell him to
stop doing that sort of shit.*

Huffing out long breaths, Peni made his way through the
bedroom quickly. His goat was getting distracted again,
making noises about their mate's scent, and Peni didn't
need to hear it. Mates were special. Yes, he knew that.
But his goat had become deluded if he thought they were
giving up the small amount of food he could afford in
a week, just because his goat wanted him on his knees
serving snacks to a demon.

You know you want to.

No, I don't. Oh, my gods. Look at this mess! Peni pointed at the state of the bathroom. *He's had a darn party in here. How else could he get water all up the walls, all over the mirror... look at that glass shower door! There're watermarks everywhere.*

Applying his cloth, Peni started rubbing—watermarks were so annoying, and if they were left to dry for long periods of time, they got even harder to remove. He kicked the towel that had been left on the floor to one side, rubbing at more marks as he silently cursed under his breath.

I know how he put those marks there.

"I don't want to hear it," Peni muttered, still rubbing madly.

I bet he caught a whiff of our wonderful scent when he came into the house, and he just had to strip off and plunge into a shower before coming out and stroking that loooooooong length, desperately panting for relief, water going everywhere as his cock jerks and spasms in his hand...

Will you shut up! Now Peni couldn't get the picture of that out of his head. *Honestly, you should come with a mute switch.*

Hey, his goat protested. *You were the one reading about all those sexy demons in that book you got from the library.*

That was fiction. This is the real life where I have to spend time on my day off scrubbing watermarks off every surface because the demon couldn't clean up after himself. Admittedly, Peni didn't have anything else to do, but it was the principle of the thing.

Peni was scrubbing the last marks off the shower glass door when the goat spoke up again. *So, about the menu for the demon's dinner tonight…*

We're having sandwiches. One sandwich. Bread and butter and a smear of honey. That's it. Peni could make his pizza last three meals if it didn't have to be shared with a demon. *Besides, there's a good chance he won't even come home tonight. Dakata rarely did on the weekend.*

Sitting back on his heels, Peni studied the pristine glass with a sigh. That was the only issue with glass—it showed every droplet. But at least he could take comfort from the fact it could be clean all weekend if Dakata or that other demon didn't come home.

Gathering up his things and the used towel, he slowly made his way to the top of the stairs when a sudden noise made him freeze. *He can't be home already. Oh, my goodness. Oh, my goodness.* Taking care to run as lightly as possible, Peni dashed down the stairs, hurrying directly to the laundry.

He came to a skidding stop, his worn sneakers sliding on the tiles as he saw the same demon, in human form this time, leaning on the cupboard door—the one where he was supposed to make his escape through.

"Hey there." The demon's eyes seemed to scorch through his clothes as they raked up and down his body. "I apologize for the mess in the bathroom."

"No problem." Peni forced himself to keep breathing, his heart pounding so hard that half of the town could probably hear it. "I'll… er… I'll just put these things away and get out of your way."

"I don't think so." Was the demon purring at him? It sure sounded like it. "The name's Merihem, and I understand we might have a bit of a connection. Did you want to go out for a meal tonight and talk about it?"

"Tonight?" Peni's eyes darted all around the room, but he doubted he could move anywhere fast enough to make his escape. *He's Dakata's guest. Maybe Merihem doesn't realize I'm not supposed to be here. I could…*

"Did you have something else to do tonight? Meeting someone else, for instance." The purr now had a very distinct rumble.

Peni gulped. "No. Nothing else. Just… you know. A sandwich and reading a book." He tried for a casual laugh, but it came off as more of a squeak. "I don't usually go out much. I… my budget, you know. Have to watch every cent."

A hint of a frown passed over Merihem's face, but it cleared just as quickly. "My treat," he insisted, and just as Peni was about to refuse a second time, the huge demon in his smart shirt and pants held out a single rose that had just appeared in his hand. "Let's start with lunch," he suggested, "and we can make our dinner plans from there."

It's just like a scene out of that book you read. Say yes. Say yes! His goat was almost leaping out of his skin as Peni shoved the towel on the counter to reach over and take the flower with trembling fingers. It was a beautiful deep red rose with soft, velvety petals.

"Thank you. Yes, all right," he whispered. "Let's start with lunch." What did he have to lose, right? Peni figured he could always find a new job and maybe even a place to stay on Monday morning. And a meal with Merihem had to be better than a sandwich?

Ask him how the bathroom walls got so dirty. His goat was beside himself with excitement. *Go on. Ask him.*

Smiling tightly, ignoring his animal spirit and Merihem's heated gaze, Peni put away his cleaning things, threw the dirty towel in the washing hamper, placed his flower in a glass with water, and then washed his hands in the laundry sink. All the while trying to figure out how he'd ended up in this situation.

"Are you ready to go?" Merihem held out his hand as Peni put the towel he'd used to dry his hands back on its railing.

"I guess I am." Peni took the hand, ignoring the shiver up his arm at the feel of Merihem's skin touching his, letting Merihem lead him back through the kitchen and out of the house.

The bedroom's the other way, his goat bleated as Merihem closed the front door after them.

Chapter Seven

Merihem

The flower... his demon was having way too much fun. He'd materialized the rose without allowing Merihem to have a say. He hadn't missed how Peni had stroked the petals or sniffed the bud.

Okay, you win, it worked, so stop gloating.

You're welcome.

When he'd watched those little fingers stroke a petal, Merihem had gotten all sorts of ideas about what Peni might like to stroke instead. His usual go-to was sexy talk. His demon had gagged him, literally, when he was about to make a suggestive comment.

He doesn't want that type of talk. He reads. None of your other bed partners read!

Merihem wanted to argue, but it was pointless when all his other instincts said Peni was special, whether that was because he was a blissful one or not, didn't seem to matter. One touch of the roughened palm against his and Merihem was ready to beg for Peni to be his. Strange, but true.

So here he was taking the pocket-sized rocket out for lunch after seeing that suggesting dinner had been a mistake when it could have given Peni time to rethink the situation. Lunch seemed like the best idea. They could most definitely extend that to dinner.

My idea.

Shut up. Merihem grumbled.

"Erm… have you changed your mind? If you have, that's fine, a sandwich will work for me." The hand holding his, the fingers released.

Fix it. Fix it now.

"Not at all, my demon half is being a little tricky," he explained, happy to cast the blame in that direction.

Peni gave a mournful sigh. "I know what you mean. My goat is also being difficult. He also isn't shutting up, and the suggestions he's making…"

Merihem glanced sideways at Peni while they strolled down the street towards a little Italian restaurant he'd eaten at with Dakata that was good, seeing his cheeks go deep pink. "Suggestions," he asked, offering a big encouraging smile.

"You don't want to know," Peni replied, the sun high-lighting strands of hair that looked like spun gold.

"Oh, but I do, I want to know everything." He added enough of a sexy growl to his words to make his point.

The blush deepened, and Peni looked anywhere but at him. "It's just silliness." He brushed a hand through his hair, glancing about nervously, chewing his lower lip between his teeth.

"I like silly," he replied, becoming more intrigued by what the little goat was saying. "But, anyway, we're here." Merihem stopped at one of the outdoor tables by the main doors into the restaurant. "Do you prefer to eat inside or out?"

"You're letting me choose?" Peni's wide-eyed look of amazement gave Merihem a swift kick to his balls, much like Peni's goat had done.

He couldn't resist and ran a finger down the warm, silky skin of Peni's cheek. "Of course, it's a date."

"Ohhh... like a real date? Where there's an expectation for kissing?" Peni slapped his forehead, and Merihem's lips quivered as he resisted chuckling, getting the impression Peni had not meant to say that.

"Yes," Merihem leaned forward as a server approached, and he bent to whisper in Peni's ear, "I was hoping for a kiss this time, but to my lips, not my balls."

Back was the adorable blush as Peni coughed and turned his attention to the server, who asked, "Table for two?"

"Please, and could we have that one there tucked in the corner?" Merihem wasn't a romantic, but he could see that was the best table.

It had a canopy over their heads if it should rain. The sky was bright, and it was warm, but one never knew in the human realm. It also had flowers creeping up the trellis that enclosed the small seating area so it would smell pleasant and not of car fumes. All these things mattered… didn't they?

"Of course," the server replied, moving towards the table and pulling out a seat for Peni.

Merihem gave the dude a hard stare, wanting to bash the guy for doing what he wanted to do for Peni. *What's wrong with me?*

Blissful one.

"Can I get you some drinks first?"

"I don't know what there is?" Peni gave the server a lost look.

"What do you like?" Merihem asked Peni, giving the server a steely-eyed glare.

"Juice."

"We'll have two orange juices, please." Merihem waited until the server scurried off before placing a hand over the back of Peni's chair in a protective move as he scanned the area.

Being outside and on display made him cautious for reasons he suspected had everything to do with Peni. Dakata had gotten all protective over Silas, his blissful one, so he figured it was that making him feel… off.

Merihem picked up the menu that was sitting on the table and offered it to Peni. "I know you like pizza, but the pasta here is wonderful." He was killing this dating lark.

Peni took the menu and eyed it, as a frown tugged at his brows.

"What's wrong?" Merihem asked, his stomach sinking.

Peni cast him a shy look. "Everything is so expensive."

His suspicions about what was happening with Dakata's housekeeper had driven Merihem to the office this morning. He wanted to snoop when no one was there and he'd found the household accounts, which displayed the name of the very female housekeeper and the extortionate amount she got paid. The clothes Peni wore were threadbare in places, something Merihem noted without it sinking in until last night when he'd had time to think about all things Peni. His mention of how little he had to spend added to the picture he was being taken advantage of.

Merihem plucked the menu from Peni's hand, giving him an encouraging smile. "Are you vegetarian?" The lack of meat on the pizza suggested he could be.

"Yes."

Merihem eyed the menu. Was it romantic to order food on a date? "Are you a picky eater?" He glanced over the top of the menu.

"No. I can't afford to be picky," Peni said quietly, squirming a little in his seat.

Using the arm that remained on the back of Peni's seat to give his blissful one a gentle squeeze of his shoulder, Merihem went back to looking at the menu. "Let's start with a tomato salad, followed by a mushroom risotto, and then we can see if we have room for dessert."

Merihem, once Peni nodded, albeit reluctantly, waited for the server who was coming with their drinks and ordered the meal.

Are you sure you made the right choices?

It's all vegetarian. Merihem started to doubt himself as the server walked off. "You do like those things, don't you?"

"Why wouldn't I?" Peni asked, the frown back. "I'm sure they'll be delicious." His cute button nose wrinkled. "The smells coming from inside are wonderful."

See, he was killing this dating thing. And if Merihem wanted meatballs, well, he'd make the sacrifice until he knew if eating meat would offend his blissful one.

Soft music filled the silence between them. Merihem ignored the traffic noise. Peni looked around, taking an interest in everything nearby.

Merihem's attention was all on the tiny man next to him. "When did Mrs. Danials get you to start doing her work for her?"

Peni, who'd reached for his glass of orange juice, jerked, and it splashed him and the table.

Why did you do that? Help him.

Merihem resisted—just—shrinking under the reprimand, feeling like a tool for blurting it out like that. He grabbed the serviettes and helped Peni wipe up the spillage. "Sorry, I burst out that out like that."

"I... you... oh, dear..."

Merihem took the soggy serviettes and plonked them at the edge of the table, hating Peni's forlorn look. "It's okay," he reassured. When that didn't remove the look, his demon started fussing.

Before the demon could decide to take matters into its own hands, Merihem plucked Peni off the seat. He weighed nothing. That was how it seemed to Merihem. He carefully arranged the gawping man on his lap, patting his back.

Be careful. You might hurt him.

How? I'm being gentle.

He was, wasn't he? Doing his best to use none of his strength, he stopped patting and opted for stroking just in case. That wouldn't hurt, would it?

He didn't want to hurt Peni. "I'm not hurting you, am I?" he asked like a complete ass, but Peni was still staring with those enormous eyes at him.

He wasn't moving, that couldn't be good.

"I..." he scratched at his head. "No one..." More scratching. "I've never sat on someone's lap before." He seemed so pleased to have gotten all his words out based on the smile he gave Merihem.

Only Merihem was too busy bristling at thoughts of Peni sitting on anyone but him. *He said he's never sat on someone. Give over, talk to him.*

"Do you like it?" Merihem asked, because he was stupid and hadn't allowed his brain to catch up with his stupid self.

"Well..." Peni gave him a thoughtful look, his cheeks were getting back to the adorable pink from before. "Yes... it's nice. You're comfortable."

Comfortable?

What the ever-loving fuck does that mean? *Comfortable!*

The server came and didn't bat an eye at them as he placed the salads down on the table. Merihem inhaled the scent of fresh herbs and balsamic vinegar.

"That looks yummy." Peni glanced from Merihem to his seat. "Wouldn't it be easier if I sat on that seat?"

The idea of letting go didn't sit well with Merihem, who was back to feeling... threatened. "We'll manage," he murmured, looking about surreptitiously, trying to figure out what was giving him the tingling bad vibes. He couldn't see anything out of the ordinary, but something was decidedly off.

He moved Peni so his legs dangled over Merihem's thighs and tucked him closer to his body to free up his arms. His next inhalation was a mix of the herbs and Peni's scent which was a little fruity. Desire tightened his groin, and he did his best to ignore it.

It was going to be a long lunch...

He reached for the cutlery and cut a decent-sized mouthful of tomato and salad, dipping it in the vinaigrette dressing. He offered the first bite to Peni. His lips parted and Merihem and his demon half both groaned.

A very long lunch.

Needing a distraction, Merihem went back to the conversation he'd started. "You work for Mrs. Danials, don't you?"

Peni sighed. "You're gonna sack me, aren't you?"

"What… why would I do that? Although being my blissful one, you really don't need to worry about working, I'm more than capable of taking care of you."

"Blissful one," he bleated.

Chapter Eight

Peni

Peni was all kinds of confused. He was sitting on the man—demon, not next to him, but actually on him, eating food that cost more than his food budget for a week.

To add sauce to that confusion, Merihem started talking about Mrs. Danials, and Peni was so sure no one was ever supposed to find out about that. He'd been so careful, and Mrs. Danials had promised repeatedly she wouldn't say anything. Now he didn't know what that meant for him in terms of his job or a place to stay.

But when he asked about being fired, Merihem threw the term 'blissful one' into the mix, and Peni was sure his brain was as mushy as the tomatoes in his salad drizzled in the vinaigrette.

"My goat told me you were my mate," he said cautiously.

"Blissful one for demons, mate for cute little goats. Same thing." Merihem seemed pleased with himself, at least, that's what his tone suggested. It's not like Peni could really see his face.

He reached for his fork, needing something to do with his hands, and stabbed a bit of salad to nibble on. He then tried to think of what to say next. Merihem gave off an air of being totally confident about everything, which was a bit intimidating.

"If it's the same thing, wouldn't you call me a mate?"

"I can call you mate if you like. But for my demon, you are a blissful one. Not many demons get one of those, you know."

No, Peni didn't know. Hoping Merihem wouldn't notice, he put his hand under the table and quickly pinched his leg.

Nope.

That hurt. He was awake.

"Do you always pinch yourself when you're on a date?"

"I don't... This is... I've never dated." Peni stuffed his mouth full of some of the salad leaves to stop himself from saying anything else silly.

"This will be the best date ever, then." Merihem sounded pleased about that, and Peni wondered why. Perhaps he'd had terrible experiences with dates before. "Because you're my blissful one, sorry, mate, if you prefer, you won't have to work. I can take care of everything."

"Won't have to work?" Peni dropped his fork, causing it to clatter on the table. He twisted, trying to see Merihem's face. "Who will clean Mr. Dakata's house?"

"It's not Dakata's house anymore. He lives with Silas in the forest. He gave the house to me. I've been called in to watch over his siblings, who are running most of his businesses now."

There was something off about that statement—not a lie exactly, but not the full truth, either. Peni decided he'd ask about that later. He was more worried about his job.

"Don't you need a house cleaner?" Peni really liked his job. He had a routine and everything.

"From what I saw this morning, the house account shows the place already has a drastically overpaid cleaner. But as I haven't seen her since I've been staying at the house, I'm beginning to think the sixty dollars an hour she's being paid is excessive, don't you? I mean, I know demons have to pay extra for staff—some people don't realize we're just like other people, but expecting people to do the work they're paid for isn't a big ask."

"Sixty dollars an hour!" Peni choked on a bit of salad caught in the back of his throat and reached for his juice, taking a quick sip. "No wonder she can afford to live in Florida. She's only paying me twenty." And then, realizing what he'd said, he added quickly, "Sorry. I mean, Mrs. Danials is visiting her sister in Florida. Visiting, she's visiting. She said her sister was sick."

"Hmm." Merihem's demon was grumbling—it was a lower tone than Merihem's. "How many hours a week do you work?"

"Forty. I've been really careful with the money. I put most of it away so I can afford a better place. I don't have references, so landlords expect more cash upfront from people like me." Peni wanted to sink into the chair with embarrassment.

Merihem's frown deepened. "And how long has Mrs. Danials been visiting her sister?"

"Four months." Peni wanted to slink off the seat and hide under the table when Merihem pulled a phone out of his shirt pocket and started tapping on the screen.

When he'd finished tapping, his phone dinged, and Merihem put it away. "If you let me know your account number, the amount you're entitled to will be credited to your bank this afternoon. I only worked it out roughly, not considering taxes and whatnot, but you should get about twenty-five thousand dollars or thereabouts. Scott, at the office will take care of it."

Peni swallowed hard, and then, when the lump in his throat wouldn't shift, he swallowed again. "Twenty-five thousand? Dollars?"

"Yep. Mrs. Danials had stolen from you roughly forty dollars an hour, for forty hours a week, for sixteen weeks. That's roughly twenty-five thousand. Have you finished with your salad?"

"Yes, thank you." *I have to tell him. I have to tell him.* "About that money. Don't you have to take some off for rent?"

"Rent?" Merihem chuckled. "You mean for you squatting in the basement?" A big hand landed on Peni's back, pushing him against the table. "Oops. Sorry. I didn't hurt you, did I?"

"No. I'm fine." Peni pushed himself back up into a sitting position. "I didn't have permission to live in the basement," he admitted. "I think that's a crime."

"You're right. It's criminal that you were forced to squat in the basement of a huge house you were cleaning all by yourself, being stolen from by the woman who is actually contracted for the job, to the point you couldn't afford to live anywhere else."

"I told you I was saving up so that I could make a rental deposit. I wasn't planning on living there forever."

The server picked that moment to come and collect the empty plates. "Your pasta will be about five minutes more."

Merihem just waved him off, or Peni assumed he did, he was still suffering with embarrassment.

"We need to rearrange you a bit so I can see your face. My demon tells me you're upset with me." Peni found himself lifted and spun to the side before resting back on Merihem's legs. "We don't like it when you're upset."

"I'm ashamed of how you found me, of how I've been living. Look at you." Peni tapped Merihem's chest which was covered by a beautiful crisp shirt. "You have everything. I have nothing. Now I've been fired…"

"W-what, I never said you were fired. Didn't I just arrange to have the money owed to you paid into your account, so you got the higher pay you should've been getting?"

"I'm not fired?" A ray of hope unfurled in Peni's heart. "I can still work at cleaning the house?"

"No. You're my blissful one. We—that's me and my demon—have to take care of you, which means you have to come with me when I'm doing my business. Someone else can clean the house."

"Mrs. Danials is in Florida." Peni's heart sank.

"Mrs. Danials' ass is fired. She knew what she was doing was wrong, and if I ever see her again…"

The demon was getting really rumbly now and Peni got the idea that could be terrible news in a restaurant.

Make him feel better. His goat piped up. *Rub his nipples.*

I'm not rubbing his nipples, but Peni did pat Merihem's chest in what he hoped was a soothing manner. The rumbles calmed down, so it must've worked.

"That feels nice." Okay, so yes, the demon was feeling better, but Merihem was still frowning. "Look, I think we're really lucky as a couple. I mean, when Dakata found his blissful one, Silas was tied to a tree. Not literally, thank goodness, although that could be fun, but he's a dryad, so neither one of them can leave the tree for long. That would drive me up the wall in a week.

"But see, you and me, this is perfect. You're homeless, well, living in a basement, but that's the same thing, so you can move up into the house with me. And you don't have to work, because I can take care of everything you need. Wherever I go, you will, too. Won't that be fun? I am rocking this dating business. Just rocking it."

Peni had a sinking feeling in his stomach. "I really like working in the house. What will I be doing while you're doing your business things?"

"You'll be with me." Merihem was smiling wide enough to show his teeth. "You can sit on my lap while I take meetings, looking cute, just like you are now. Perfect."

"Just sitting, looking cute." Peni inhaled sharply. "I don't think I'll be very good at doing that."

Don't do it. Don't even think it. He's our mate.

His goat could sense what he was planning before he'd even formed a coherent thought. Because Peni knew if his mate did not respect him, there wasn't going to be a mating. Merihem could afford all the fancy shirts he liked, but Peni had his pride. "Can I get up for a moment, please?"

"Sure. But just for a moment. I like you there." Merihem was all smiles as he pushed back his chair. Peni slid off his lap. "Did you get a crick in your leg? I get funny aches like that sometimes. Usually, when I've been seriously kicking some demon ass." Merihem laughed. Peni didn't think he was funny.

"No. No crick." Turning and facing the demon, just out of arm's reach, Peni pushed back his goat's bleating and dug deep into the last ounce of courage he had left. "I can't be with you and just sit on your lap while you run your business. I'm not a pet. I'm a person. I have wants, needs, dreams, and desires, just like the next person, and unlike the Mrs. Danials of this world, I'm prepared to work for what I have."

"You don't have to. I can take care of you." Merihem wasn't smiling now.

"I'm sure you can. But your comments, and how you view our life together puts you in the same league as my father, who thought my looks and where I put my cock were the only things important about me, too. I didn't join in my father's orgies, and I'm not sitting on your leg, keeping your cock warm either. Thank you for the salad."

"Who said anything about orgies? I'm not taking you to any orgies. Peni. Peni?"

Peni turned and started to walk away briskly, his goat bleating in his ear all the while. *Yes, I know he's our mate, but he's a self-centered asshole. I won't… I can't…*

He met the server coming to the table with their pasta. "Shall I just leave this on the table for you?"

"Yes, thank you." Peni was sure Merihem could eat his portion, too. He quickened his step. He had to get back to the house before Merihem did so he could clear his things out of the basement. *I'm going to have to leave town… I'm going to have to find somewhere else to stay… I don't know what to do.* The only thing Peni knew was he was destined for better things than sitting on someone's lap and looking pretty.

A tremendous roar sounded behind him, and Peni turned, just for a second, to see Merihem's demon fighting past the server, coming in his direction. The roars were full of anger, and for the first time in ages, Peni and his goat were in accord.

Run.

Chapter
Nine

Merihem

Merihem's mouth had run away with him, or so it seemed. He wasn't sure how he'd got painted into such a tight corner. Now he was in trouble because his blissful one was hightailing down the street.

What were you thinking? His demon roared and the next thing he knew, he was naked and running down the street chasing his little goat, who was fast on his feet. However, his legs were much shorter than Merihem's demon.

I was trying to make amends for that woman taking advantage of Peni. That's what I was thinking.

You weren't thinking at all while mouthing off about him sitting pretty on your knee. Can't you see he takes pride in what he does? You have to ask what he wants.

The roaring was deafening as the sound of brakes slamming and metal crunching was lost on his demon, who could see exactly where Peni ran to—Dakata's house.

If he runs away, I'm going to cause a riot that will give the king a genuine reason to boot us to the darkest pits of hell.

Shut up and let me think.

Fuck no, if you think we'll end up losing the one precious gift Fate has given us. You keep your mouth shut and let me do the talking.

Yeah, you're making such a good impression. A bare-assed demon roaring for all his worth. That'll work to make Peni want us.

The roaring ceased, but Merihem wasn't sure if that was because they could see Peni skid to a stop at Dakata's door and dart around the side of the building towards the window he used to get in and out unnoticed.

He didn't get a chance to think what he should do as they watched Peni's ass disappear through the open window. There was no way they could fit in there.

If we go in through the house, he'll run out this way. If he knows we're here, then he's gonna go the other way.

The entire world knows where we are! How could they not? A big red assed demon with his cock slapping off his thigh, his horns glowing in the sunlight. *No one would notice that, would they?*

Sarcasm was all Merihem had in his panic. He didn't want to lose the most precious gift he'd received. Hell no, but he'd got lost in how wonderful it was to have Peni so close to him. He could easily envision Peni being there with him—all the time. And maybe talking wasn't his strong suit, but shouldn't he get points for trying?

His demon rolled his eyes at him and punched a vast hole next to the window. Brick and dust flew as the wall crumbled like a sandcastle a random child had whacked with a spade.

Dakata's gonna have our ass for this!

We'll fix it. His demon side didn't sound in the least bit concerned as he ducked in through the hole and gave the wide-eyed Peni a gentle smile. "Sorry for making such a dramatic entrance, but I was worried you'll run before we had a chance to meet, officially." His voice was deeper and smooth as damn silk. He offered his enormous hand to Peni. "Hi, I'm Merihem's better half."

Merihem gave a dramatic eye roll at his demon side.

"W-Well... I-I... W-Wow, you're big." Peni didn't move as he eyed the hand that was bigger than his head.

His demon smiled widely. "Thank you, blissful one."

The hand holding the book dropped to Peni's side and his tiny shoulders sagged when he glanced at the hole, and then at the dirty floor. "You've made a mess. Who's gonna clean that up now everyone is fired?"

Why does he keep focusing on cleaning?

Shut up and let me figure this out. You've already proven to be inept.

His demon lowered himself to the ground, uncaring that he sat on a pile of rubble. Peni watched the move but stayed right where he was. "What my human side was trying to do, and failing miserably at, was to explain that if you didn't want to work from now on, you don't have to. We would like to take care of you. Make you feel special."

Merihem bristled. *I didn't fail.*

Shut up. Look, he's thinking.

Merihem couldn't argue with his demon. Peni was giving them a thoughtful look. "So are you saying that you aren't going to choose what I do…" he sucked on his lower lip, his gorgeous skin back to the pretty pink. "That you see that sitting on your knee looking"—he waved the book about, and Merihem grinned—"whatever you said."

"Of course, the choice is yours." The demon patted his bare thigh. "I won't say that you sitting right here isn't very appealing. I won't lie. But you are free to choose what you want to do. No restrictions. We have more than enough to share with you, so that gives you options."

"Options." His brows were back tugging together and Merihem felt panic. His demon side held him back. *Give him a chance to finish.* "I've never had options before." A very tiny curve of his lips and Merihem became enchanted. "What would that entail… my options, I mean." He blushed, his gaze dropping to their lap before slipping away.

"Can I ask what you envisioned for yourself?"

Still taller than Peni, his demon maintained eye contact by craning his neck. It wasn't really comfortable, but as Peni hadn't attempted to flee, they remained as they were.

Back to chewing the lower lip, the one Merihem was desperate to taste, Peni eyed them thoughtfully. The plump lip popped out. "I love books… all books. The library is my most favorite place. I enjoy cleaning, too. It's orderly. I like order. My father had so many orgies at the house, making things always messy with… *stuff everywhere.*"

And we're back to the orgies!

Give over, weren't you listening? He didn't want any part in them.

Alright, keep your hair on. So what does he mean by stuff?

How would I know? And be quiet. Can't you see we're making progress? I want a kiss too!

"So working in a library would suit you?" The head shake confused them. "You don't want that?"

"No, it's not that I don't want that. You need a degree in Library Science to work in a library."

Really?

Oh, that plan of yours just fell flat. Look how sad he looks now. Merihem felt like they were taking steps back and forth, then side to side, and it was making him feel dizzy.

I've got it. "Do you want to go to college?"

The slow blink Peni gave them was adorable. "I can't afford that."

His demon offered his hand once more and smiled softly, or at least tried. "You are our blissful one—mate, that I believe means the same thing." A small nod. "What we have is yours. You can afford to do anything you want." He wiggled his fingers. "Anything. That includes college or staying in our home and cleaning, reading, and doing whatever you do to fill your day. Or the option of coming with us and sitting with us, that's there, too. But from this moment forward, the choice is yours to have. We hope you'll choose us because we'll cherish you for the rest of eternity."

Peni's pretty colored cheeks came with parted lips and a dazed expression. The hand remained in the air. They waited.

Does he believe us?

Of course he does, mates and blissful ones don't tell lies to each other. So once we've cleaned up the mess you made. You'll need to explain why you're really here, in the human realm.

The rough pads of his fingers sliding against their skin stopped the internal conversation. His demon side didn't so much as move a muscle as Peni inched closer, his palm sliding against theirs. The roughness sent tingles to parts of them that made it hard to stay on track—at least for Merihem.

"You won't force me to pick something I don't want?" he asked seriously.

They nodded. "Never. The choice is yours." His demon and Merihem were in total agreement.

Peni made a small sound that sounded like a cough and a bleat.

His goat's happy. You did it.

Were you in doubt?

"I like sitting on your lap... just so you know, only I wouldn't want to do that all the time." Peni gave them a shy look from under his eyelashes, inching a little closer. "But before I do that again, could you put some pants on?"

One thought resolved that issue. "Do you want to sit on my lap now? Cuddle me? I was a little worried earlier we'd lose you, so a cuddle would be lovely."

Lovely? What...

There was the tiniest hesitation before Peni's fingers clung to Merihem's demon's hand, and he allowed them to guide him down onto their thighs. His little arms trled to reach up around their neck to give them a hug. He huffed in pure frustration and wriggled, making Merihem curse and his demon side moan, their body heating.

"You're huge," Peni panted and then shifted his legs so that they were now facing each other, him straddling their lap.

Oh, to the Demon King.

His hands slide around their rib cage, and Peni nestled right in, shuffling his ass to remove the gap between them. He snuffled and bleated before he murmured, "Is this okay?"

"Y-Yep."

Is that all you've got?

He's hugging us. He's touching us.

Like I can miss that.

Roughened palms ran up their skin, not far, as his arms were too short, but it was amazing. It wasn't all about the tingles of desire that came with the touch, no it was the act. The gentle way Peni held him offered something Merihem had never asked for in his long life: affection. The simplicity of it captured his heart as it beat that much harder.

Peni's head tilted back to glance up. "Your heart's racing. Are you okay?" His brows pinched.

"I am overwhelmed." They answered honestly, his demon had never been a game player.

His plump lips parted, and for the longest moment, they stared at each other. Emotions swirled in the depths of Peni's eyes. His demon lowered his head until their lips were nearly touching. Soft breaths caressed their skin as they held still, waiting for Peni to decide what he wanted.

Then everything faded away. The gentle touch of skin on skin was all there was. The merest of touches that made Merihem's world shrink to the most important thing in the universe—Peni.

Chapter Ten

Peni

It was Monday morning. The demon, Merihem, was back at work, and Peni was cleaning, headphones on, music blaring in his ears. Merihem's demon hadn't wanted to go, but Peni was quietly persuasive. "I need time to think about our next steps," he said firmly, buoyed by the weekend's events.

The hole in the wall of the basement had been fixed. Apparently, demons could just think things, and they happened, which Peni thought was rather cool.

The rest of Saturday and all of Sunday, the demon followed Peni around the house, zapping up food when Peni mentioned he was hungry and doing more listening than talking, which went a long way to helping Peni feel a little less crowded, even if physically he was. He still got the idea the demon was hiding something from him, but then he reasoned if he had trust issues, it was only fair to allow the demon his as well.

Their one point of contention was when Peni went to sleep downstairs on Saturday night. The demon absolutely did not want him in the basement, and they made grumbled threats of creating another hole in the wall. To keep the structural integrity of Dakata's house intact, Peni agreed to sleep on the couch in the living room.

It was no surprise that the demon was half-wedged in the same space when he woke up. The demon's skin was surprisingly warm. Sunday night he got the demon to lie down first, and then he snuggled in beside him. It was the best sleep he'd ever had. Those huge arms and wide chest were amazing. Better than any pillow, although he'd never say that aloud.

Merihem himself emerged on Monday morning, looking a bit sheepish and also very smart and confident in his suit. "You should let me stay with you. I'm not trying to force you to do something you don't want to do, but what if something happens while I'm away?"

"I've been cleaning the house for four months, and no one has ever come here during the day except you. Now off you go," Peni felt like a housewife, shooing his mate out the door.

"I'll be back at lunchtime." Merihem was dragging his feet. "I'll take you out somewhere nice for lunch."

"Thank you, dear." Peni smiled up at him and accepted the kiss offered, although he could feel how badly both man and demon wanted more. "Have a nice day."

Closing the door, Peni sighed, although it wasn't with relief. *How weird is it that I miss him already, and he's barely down the road? No. No. This won't do. Monday is clean the kitchen day. Let's get on with it.*

His goat, who'd been remarkably quiet over the weekend, piped up less than half an hour after Merihem had gone. *You sent our mate out into the world horny and without any relief. That's not what a good mate does. What if he finds someone else to polish his schlong?*

Then he's not our mate, in which case we won't care. Peni applied some cream cleaner to the counter, humming along with his music. *Mates don't cheat on each other.*

But still... that cock is a thing of beauty.

You only saw the demon dick, and I can't see that fitting inside this body anytime soon. My stomach would get pushed out of my throat.

It wasn't that Peni hadn't thought about it, over the long hours the demon had been following him around. He knew the lore about shifter mates, even if his father didn't believe in what he called "nonsense." Spunk, spit, and a bite would cement them together, and it didn't make any difference that Peni shared his spirit with a goat rather than a wolf or a bear. The rules were still the same.

What had helped, and Peni was cross with himself for even thinking it, was that the demon wouldn't let Merihem come through. "He talks shit and upsets you," the demon grumped the one time Peni asked about it. "He needs to listen to understand your needs."

Which had been a sweet thought. Peni sighed. It was funny because, in the book he had been reading, it was the demon who was the rampaging asshole who didn't care about anyone or anything. But aside from the one little rampage at Saturday's lunch, Merihem's demon genuinely seemed to care.

The issue was with the act of sex itself. Peni had never done it, never even got close. But from what he'd seen numerous times when he'd lived at home, sex was violent and noisy. There was very little caring involved, and above all, it was messy. Peni shuddered as a picture flicked into his mind. Some things could never be unseen, and he'd seen his father waving his cock around, sticking it into more holes than a hedgehog had prickles.

Focus on the task at hand. Peni used wide circular motions with his cloth to wipe off most of the cream cleaner, and then, with a second softer cloth, he buffed the counter until it shined.

I genuinely don't believe it would be like that with our mate. The goat wasn't as strident as he usually was. He'd seen the trauma Peni went through, and while he talked like a randy sailor most of the time, their bond was deep. *His kisses are nice, and he's remarkably controlled considering he spent all weekend with a rock-hard dick.*

So did I most of the time. Peni could be honest with himself, if no one else. *It's not that I don't want to. It's just that I'm scared. What if...*

"You good-for-nothing piece of shit. You stole my job from me." Peni ducked as a hand came out of nowhere, knocking his headphones clear off his head.

"Mrs. Danials." Peni backed up, clutching his cloth to his chest as he faced five-foot-ten worth of fury in a blue and white dress. "What are you doing here? I thought you were in Florida."

"Yes, you thought that didn't you, you slimy piece of shit. And you thought you could slink your sexy ass up against that fucking demon, telling lies about me and getting me fired. You stole my job!"

"I haven't talked to Mr. Dakata." Peni's back was hard against the stove, but the woman was still coming towards him. "I did what you said. I only worked between eight and four when Mr. Dakata was at work. I've never spoken to him. I haven't."

"Then how come I had a lawyer fella turning up at my sister's house over the weekend, no less?" Mrs. Danial's face twisted with rage. "Serving me papers. Embarrassing me in front of my family. Accusing me of theft! I never stole anything from nobody."

"But... but..." Peni shook his head so hard his brain rattled. "I didn't do anything. I was just cleaning—"

"Cleaning, my ass. Did you get tired of scrubbing floors for a living and thought you would weasel your way into the demon's bed? Sucking cock as a sideline now, you little whore?"

"I haven't said anything. I haven't lied." Peni ducked as a huge bag came towards his head.

"I gave you a chance." The bag connected, and Peni's goat bleated as pain shot down his neck. "I took you off the streets." Another whack. "I took your sorry ass in when no one else would even look at you, and this is how you repay me?"

The whacks were coming hard and fast. Peni wouldn't hit back. He'd never hit a woman, but as he crouched down, trying to protect his head and stomach, Mrs. Danials was relentless. All he could think as the woman used him as a punching bag, was would she kick him out of the house before Merihem came back for lunch, or was she going to leave his dead ass on the kitchen floor? *How can I call him… Would he even come when I didn't have sex with him?*

A demon roar reverberated around the kitchen, rattling the pots and the windows.

He came…

Chapter Eleven

Merihem

"Christa, I said no. The notes that Dakata left clearly state the terms of the contract for Live & Die mean they have to play those ten dates. They can't now decide to do two less because one of the band has met someone and wants to stay in a city for a few extra days getting his cock sucked."

Christa rolled her eyes at him, then turned to Scott, who had come in to take notes of the meeting. "He's got no heart."

"I've plenty of heart," Merihem growled, though his lips curved into a small smile at how big his heart felt around Peni. His little goat was a pocket rocket. He was full of energy and although he'd had his ass curtailed over the weekend by his demon, he'd still had fun.

He moved his head from side to side, feeling the stiffness in his neck. He was far too big to be sleeping on a couch. Not that he'd complain when Peni decided last night he was better than a mattress and used them.

"Are you even listening to me?" Christa snapped, drawing his attention to the stunning woman, eyeing him funnily. "You've a dopey look on your face. What's with you?"

She glanced at Scott who remained poised waiting for them to continue, nothing about his expression gave away his thoughts. "There's something up with him, you see it?"

Scott remained silent.

Christa huffed, fluffing her hair. "Demons!"

"You do know you are one?" Merihem pointed out, amused. Then he got a sharp unexpected tug in the center of his chest. He gasped, and his demon side became alert.

Peni.

Peni.

They said together.

They were up and out of the chair so fast it fired back and hit the wall. Dust bloomed in the air, but in the blink of an eye, they were inside Dakata's home.

His demon emerged as they stood and listened in the hallway, sensing where their blissful one was. Then they heard screeching, "I took your sorry ass in when no one else would even look at you, and this is how you repay me?" The sound of whacking followed, and then painful whimpers.

Naked, roaring, his demon in an absolute fury like they'd never experienced before—and that was saying something—they ran in the direction of the sounds.

Their eyes narrowed on the horror who dared to hit their blissful one with a large bag while he cowered in pain and fear on the floor. Any reason, calm or negotiation skills left for the demon realm as Merihem's two halves were in total agreement. His enormous fist reached for the woman and with a muttering of an incantation—one he shouldn't use because he was no longer Controller, but he couldn't give two flying fucks right then—he sent her to hell. Death was too easy for her when he could see the bruises forming right in front of his eyes on Peni's pale skin.

"You came," Peni whisper-sobbed.

Their hands were shaking with the adrenaline and the need to punch something. They took a breath, then another before they could get their lips to work. "Always," he rasped.

Peni bleated and jumped up and on him. The unexpected move had them land hard on their tailbone to catch him. He nestled his face right into the crook of Merihem's demon's neck, kissing the bounding pulse rocketing against the skin. "You came," he said again, hot breath brushing over his sensitive skin that burned from the rage. "No one's ever protected me before." His tiny arms clutched at his neck. Awe, it came at them in a massive dollop and would have knocked them right back onto their ass if they'd been standing when the hot lips repeatedly kissed his neck.

A lump developed in Merihem's throat at the emotions Peni wasn't shy about sharing. The anger drained away as he held on to their blissful one, inhaling the scent of cleaning products and Peni's sweet smell. "I'll always come. Nothing would stop me, not even death."

Peni shuddered, and the lips stilled. "No talk of death, okay?" His head popped back and the bruising and swelling to the left eye, along with the mark on his cheek, brought back the fury. "What did you do to Mrs. Danials?"

Merihem growled at thoughts of going to Hell and—

"Oh, dear, what did you do?" Peni's work-roughened palms slid from around his neck to cup his cheeks. "She was awful, no doubt… but…"

"Awful. She hit my blissful one." His finger trembled—and he had no shame about that when it came to Peni—while he traced the delicate, puffy skin by his teary eye. "Awful doesn't even come close to what she is." Except Merihem wasn't going to say what he thought aloud, his little goat didn't need to hear those obscenities.

"She was upset you fired her," Peni explained as they wiped a tear off his cheek. "It's all my fault."

With their heart slamming against their ribs at the glistening eyes, they came forward, and their forehead's touched. The size difference made it hard not to overpower Peni, but they tried. "She deserved it. Because she is nothing but a thief and a liar. She took advantage of you. You are not to take the blame for that."

Peni got that thoughtful expression, the one that said he was thinking before answering, so they waited and took comfort from the closeness.

We should never have left him. See, my idea about him sitting on our lap would have prevented this from happening.

Shut up.

His demon side was struggling to not agree, Merihem felt it. *We need to find a solution to make sure this doesn't happen again.*

Agreed.

"You're right. She had no right to hit me." Peni's smooth forehead rubbed against theirs. They got a hard blast of feels at the gesture. "But you didn't answer my question. What did you do with her?" His eyes searched Merihem's, looking for what they weren't sure.

"Sent her to hell so she can join those who enjoy playing hard and loose with their thoughts and fists. See how she enjoys that."

He bleat-squealed, and Merihem's demon grinned widely at the approval of their goat.

"You did?" Peni asked, his head moving back, much to their disappointment.

"It was that or crush her bones. I wasn't sure you'd like that because it would have made a mess." He blushed, like a serious heat wave at the dopey look of love that got aimed at them. *Right choice.* Merihem was grateful for his red skin, so Peni couldn't see them actually blushing. It was a little mortifying. "Anyway, this means she gets to suffer for a very long time and think over her actions for daring to harm one hair on your precious head."

Peni reached up to tug on a strand of hair. "It wasn't my hair she hurt."

They chuckled and, unable to resist the plump, pouting lips, gave Peni a tiny, delicate peck on the mouth. Or they tried.

Peni's eyes widened for a moment before his hands slipped around their neck once more. His fingers tickled the skin, then roamed up the back of his skull. Fingers playing with his locks before going to his horns. A demon's power lay in his horns. To touch them would give that power to the individual. It could also be classed as fore-play to a demon. Motionless, they stared at Peni, uncertain their little goat would be ready for the outcome. "If you touch my horns, especially the tips, I possibly—could very well—lose control."

The hands at the base of his horns hesitated and Peni's cute brows drew together. "Lose control, how?"

The innocence was easy to see because Peni wasn't a game player. Merihem and his demon both mentally pre-pared themselves. Neither wanted to frighten their bliss-ful one. "With a blissful one, I am not sure. But any touch from you ignites my blood with desires I've never experi-enced before. My horns are sacred. They hold a demon's power. No one has ever gotten to touch them intimately."

The absolute look of joy at that declaration gave Mer-ihem and his demon a boost to a certain part of their anatomy they'd been working to keep control of. Anger could arouse him, but the fear that came with thoughts of someone hurting their blissful one had put paid to that earlier.

Now, the anger, though still simmering in the background, wasn't what was stimulating him. It came from the gentle touch of Peni's hands. Things between them were swing-ing in a different direction. One he wasn't sure Peni was prepared for. His demon cock was enormous, and it would be way too much for their little goat. If Peni saw him fully aroused, he would surely run from them, so they thought about the worst hell offered Mrs. Danials, trying to control what was happening below the waistline.

Only their tiny goat had other ideas, it seemed. The next thing they were holding the cutest and smallest white goat, who bleated crazily, his tongue wiggling at their face.

Lifting him up closer, they grinned at the cutie. "Aren't you gorgeous?"

Frantic wriggling came with loud bleating that made them laugh. As they brought the goat closer, figuring that was what it wanted, when his head lowered, and his tongue came out and flicked about, almost like it was trying to…

lick them. They had no issue with that—none when he was the cutest goat they'd ever seen—their blissful one.

The second it could reach them, it lapped at their cheek, now their neck, and before they could fathom what was coming next, teeth nipped at their throat.

They groaned at a rush of fervent desire that came embarrassingly fast. His breath caught in his chest at the throbbing that spread from his aroused shaft to his balls and up his spine, making him shiver. The scent of his arousal got a weird-sounding bleating with teeth embedded in his neck.

Merihem tilted his head to the side to let the goat have better access to his throat. He squirmed at the bite becoming true. His cry was silent as his whole body spasmed at the merest contact. Desire, hot, potent, the kind that made the world spiral out of control before snapping back into place, made him gasp.

His vision blurred at the tug of teeth in his throat. His balls grew tight, and the feeling curling in the pit of his belly left them in no doubt about the fact he was going to come.

As if the tiny goat knew, teeth sank even deeper into his flesh. Merihem's large body arched, shuddered and roared, his shaft throbbed painfully before ribbons of cum fired from the leaking tip. Cum splattered everywhere, including under their blissful one's belly.

Look at what you did. You never asked if this was okay.

Merihem's demon blinked slowly, their brain fried from the unexpected events as teeth let go of his neck.

How am I supposed to look our demon in the eye? Hmm. Tell me! This is mortifying... you randy goat.

Lips twitching, he eyed the little goat, which they lowered to the floor. *We love your randy goat.*

The little goat looked up. Merihem and his demon side both agreed the crooked grin was adorable. *You can hear me?*

Yes.

It was hard to hold on to their amusement, but they managed when Peni blasted them with all his thoughts at once.

This?

How?

Oh my?

All my thoughts?

You naughty goat?

You bit him. How could you without asking?

That's not the point, is it?

This isn't funny!

Oh, to the goat gods, how can I face Merihem now?

When they stopped, Merihem shifted to look at his mate. "Peni," he murmured gently, stroking a finger over the rough hair on the back of his neck. "We each have another side that does things we don't always approve of. But they are us. And what happened between us is wonderful. I want to nibble on your neck if that makes you feel any better."

He felt the uncertainty, and then Peni shifted, sitting on the sticky, wet floor looking anything but certain. "Wonderful?" he asked, sounding doubtful as he eyed Merihem with dark shades of red slashing over his cheeks.

Bending so their noses were nearly touching, the scent of his cum lingered between them. He held Peni's gaze, wanting this to be about them, not their other halves right then. *Don't fuck up.* He ignored his demon side. "Yes. Feel our connection." He took his small hand and pressed it to the center of his chest. Letting him feel how hard his heart beat. "This beats for you and no one else. It is yours for all

eternity and beyond. Nothing will break our connection."
He rubbed their noses together, smiling shyly. "And when
you're ready to complete our bond, then all you need to
do is ask."

"Ask?" he squeaked.

Merihem kissed him because he couldn't resist, but he
kept it gentle, holding back his true passion. Peni wasn't
ready for that, not yet. His thoughts didn't hide that. "If
you can't, then that's fine, too. We'll figure it out."

His blush deepened prettily. "Ok-ay. You'll figure it out."
He'll do the figuring. Yeah, that works.

You do know he can hear us?

Well, how do we turn it off?

Chapter Twelve

Peni

There were times when Peni got overwhelmed in life. His goat was more worldly in a lot of ways. He saw things more simplistically, and that was understandable, given he was an animal at heart. Peni was the one who worried and fretted, and yes, he knew he was prone to overthinking things. But there was so much going on, his brain felt as if it was going to explode, and he now had an extra worry to add to the list—would anything in his life ever be normal again?

There was the unexpected arrival of Mrs. Danials. Peni's face was still throbbing, and it would take a long time for him to forget the hate in her voice.

And what about the lawsuit she was yelling about? Peni tried to hide his worries from Merihem. Was he going to get served papers because he'd been sleeping in the basement? The threat felt real. Not that he was sleeping down there anymore because of an even bigger change in his life.

Peni was furious, embarrassed, and completely mortified by what his goat had done. He hadn't even planned to shift. No, his goat just burst out. What was worse was that his animal side took the most serious decision a shifter could make *out of his hands* and left Peni with a mate to contend with.

A mate who was grinning at him and stroking his face, which was nice, yet… "I should probably clean something. I haven't finished the kitchen counter." Peni was doing his best to cling to what he knew.

Only before he'd finished speaking, Merihem was shaking his head. "I need to speak to Dakata, which means calling a special taxi and going to the forest."

"Yes. You should definitely do that." Peni needed time to think alone. "I'll just stay here…"

"You can't." Merihem looked aghast.

Peni flinched back as if Merihem had hit him. "I can't stay here anymore?"

"No, no. You heard me wrong. I mean, you need to be with me right now, sweetheart. Please. Come to the forest with me."

Frowning, Peni gave Merihem his best "look". "You said *you* needed to speak to Mr. Dakata. You said *you* needed to call a special taxi and go to some unnamed forest. There was nothing in what you said about me. I need to clean." *And put some clothes on,* but Peni prayed that thought hadn't gone through their weird bond. Shifting was not good on his clothes, although he had it easier than bigger shifters.

"I'm sorry." Merihem looked as if he was having an internal discussion with his demon half. Peni found that easier to spot for some reason. "I am used to… you know what? I should not fob you off with an excuse. Put bluntly, I misspoke. I meant to say it would make me very happy if you would come to the forest with me."

Peni glanced up at the kitchen counter and then back at his mate. "Are you sure I can't just stay here?" Cleaning was way easier.

"You got attacked in this house. We can't let that happen again," Merihem stressed.

"I don't think it will be a problem now Mrs. Danials is in hell." *I need to think! My brain has got some serious organizing to do.* But Peni didn't want Merihem to think he was incapable. It was bad enough that his goat had done the unthinkable, but ultimately he and his goat spirit were one. He was going to have to live with his goat's decision. The thing was, Peni, if asked, couldn't tell anyone how he felt about what was done. He had absolutely no idea. His whole life had simply spiraled out of control in a matter of hours.

Which meant all Peni could do was focus on the immediate issue. Merihem wanted to go to the forest. Peni didn't have any clothes on. "Fine. I'll go to the forest with you. Can you close your eyes, please?"

"Are you going to run away if I do?" Merihem's hands rested on his shoulders gently, his gaze revealing worry. Something else Peni was getting better at reading.

"No. I won't leave the room." Peni wiggled, trying to get free. "I just need you to close your eyes for two minutes."

"I enjoy looking at you." Merihem was grinning and probably thought he was teasing, but Peni was close to breaking point.

Reaching up, he grabbed Merihem's face and squeezed it. Not hard. He'd never hurt his mate, but enough to get his attention. "I want you to do this one thing. Let me up and close your eyes. Please."

"If you want me to close my eyes, you shouldn't be sitting on me naked."

"That wasn't intentional. I want you to close your eyes so I can get dressed." Merihem clearly didn't get it. He probably walked around all day with his cock bouncing from thigh to thigh in his human or his demon form and didn't care if people looked. Hadn't that been how they'd met in the first place? The problem was Peni wasn't like that.

"Properly," he added as Merihem closed his eyes halfway. "All the way shut."

"You're not very trusting for a blissful one," Merihem grumped, but his eyes finally closed.

Jumping up, Peni grabbed his clothes, thanking the Fates and anyone else he could think of that his goat form was so small. His clothes weren't ripped, but Peni was all fingers and thumbs trying to get them on. His pants suddenly seemed too tight, and he almost fell over, dancing on one leg, trying to get his other foot through the hole. His shirt was inside out, and Peni had no idea when that happened. That was more time needed, turning it in the right way before tugging it over his head. *Shoes. Shoes. I know I had shoes.*

Peni saw the edge of one poking out from Merihem's butt. There was no sign of the other one. *He's probably sitting on it.* "I'm dressed," he said out loud. "You can get up now."

Merihem stood up with a dancer's grace. Peni felt something stir in his lower belly, but he squashed it down. His brain was a mass of jellybeans, and none of the colors were sorted.

He darted around his mate and grabbed his shoes, sitting again so he could slide them on. He didn't want to fall over with Merihem watching. "So, what's the story with the special taxicab? Is it like Cinderella's coach and turns into a pumpkin at midnight?"

Chapter Thirteen

Merihem

He couldn't hold back his chuckle at how adorable his blissful one was. *Cinderella.* Dakata would choke on his own spit at that type of reference to him. It couldn't be Silas as it was definitely Dakata who was the one who'd run from Silas, just like the girl in the fairy tale, not the other way around.

"Where Silas and Dakata live, it's kind of secret," Merihem explained, not that it was exactly true. Otherwise, how would the rogue demons have kidnapped Wanda, Silas's sister, mistaking her for Dakata's blissful one? "There's a special taxi driver that Silas uses to take folks to the forest," he continued when Peni didn't look convinced.

"Then it's not a secret."

Back was the adorable, confused look that made Merihem click his fingers to dress to hide his reaction. Using small amounts of his magic couldn't be bad, could it?

He shook off the worry when it came to being a supportive mate to their little goat, who wasn't ready for him to be naked and fully aroused. He'd gotten some of Peni's thoughts, despite how he'd tried to keep them to himself. Scaring him was not the aim, especially when Merihem didn't miss how relieved Peni looked at him when he had clothes on. Nakedness was not something he ever concerned himself with, in fact, Merihem preferred it. He needed to make sure to remember to wear clothes with Peni—regardless of how restrictive they felt to him—when it made his blissful one happier. Why couldn't someone come up with a range of clothes that didn't feel like he had any on?

"Are we going? Or I could—"

His thoughts snapped back into focus at where Peni's opinions were about to circle back to staying home.

"Nope, staying isn't an option right now." Despite the fact that he'd dealt with Mrs. Danials, his senses were telling him to be careful. "I'll ring Scott, and he can call George."

Peni didn't look convinced, but he took Merihem's out-stretched hand and followed as Merihem retrieved his phone and called Scott. A minute later, they were waiting at the curb for the taxicab.

"So this forest, is it special?"

Merihem gave Peni a thoughtful look. "Silas is a dryad and so is his sister. They look after the forest, protect it from those silly enough not to treasure the benefits it gives to everyone."

Peni's smile was slow in coming, yet when it appeared fully, Merihem couldn't look away. The sun was bright in the sky, yet it didn't hold the same warmth as the smile Peni aimed at him. "He sounds like he does a worthwhile job."

"He does," Merihem agreed. There weren't that many dryads left in the world. Humans weren't all about un-derstanding what evolution did to the planet.

A cab pulled to a stop and Merihem bent to look in the open window, keeping hold of Peni's hand. "You, George?"

"Yep," the big guy muttered around a toothpick he had between his lips. "You Merihem?"

"I am. This is my blissful one, Peni," he announced, liking the way it sounded as he said it.

Peni made a kind of odd squealing-bleating noise as Merihem opened the door of the cab for Peni. His cheeks were a pretty pink as he slid into the cab at Merihem's gentle nudging.

On their way seconds later, Peni looked out the window, chewing on his lower lip. Merihem focused, and though it took a minute or two, he managed to figure out what was worrying Peni the most. He wasn't sure prying in his blissful one's thoughts was the done thing. He'd already gotten into enough trouble, so he debated how to approach the subject of what was playing on Peni's mind.

He lounged back on the seat, trying to make himself comfortable in the cramped space. A seven-foot dude was not meant to be squished into the back of a small taxicab. His hand touched the window Peni was looking out of.

Peni glanced back at him, the lower lip still between his teeth.

He's upset. Come on, stop dithering and fix this. I can't because I'd be worse than a sardine crammed into a can if I came out.

His demon was clearly miffed at both him and the car. *It's not dithering. I'm thinking of the best way to approach this situation.*

Before his demon could continue to give him a headache, Merihem stroked a finger over Peni's shoulder. "I'm picking up that you're worried about something. Is it some of the things Mrs. Danials threatened you with, by chance?"

Peni visibly sagged, and Merihem was back to wanting to kick that woman's ass for upsetting his blissful one. "Could I go to prison?"

At the alarm running through him at such a thought, Merihem picked Peni up, grateful he was small enough not to clout his head on the roof of the cab, before he put him in his lap. The very idea of something like that happening sent his demon into a fit of rage. "What did Mrs. Danials say to make you think that?"

Peni sighed and looked at the seat he'd been sitting on, before looking at Merihem. "Sorry, I... We... I need a hug," Merihem finished, uncaring George could hear, or if that made him sappy.

"Oh... okay." Peni came in, his arms open and then he eyed Merihem's wide shoulders. "Erm... I'm not sure..." he tilted his head this way and that, eyeing him in such a way, Merihem's heart beat a little faster.

"Yes, I've got it now." He reached up around Merihem's neck and pressed his cheek to Merihem's chest. "This work?"

The muffled question and action gave Merihem a swift thump to the center of his being. His demon made a loud sniffing noise as he blinked and wrapped his arms around Peni, careful not to squeeze too hard. "Perfect."

They sat like that, and Merihem could not remember a time he had been more… content.

"We're here," muttered George around the toothpick. "Just give me a call when you're ready to leave."

Hating he had to move, Merihem decided the back of the cramped cab actually benefited him like he'd never expected. He huffed and opened the door to lift Peni out, who now wore a curious expression as he glanced about.

Merihem paid George and gave him a nod as he grinned at the wad of cash he'd given him. Out of the cab, they didn't have to wait but a moment for Dakata to appear with Silas.

"So what disaster has befallen my business now?" Dakata asked, looking wary enough to piss Merihem off from the affront.

"Listen, it's got nothing to do with your business. But if you wanna talk about you letting things slide. How about we talk about how your housekeeper pulling a fast one on you and using my blissful one as a slave while she suns herself in Florida?"

"What," Dakata exclaimed loud enough to make Silas wince.

Silas came forward and held out his hand to Peni. "Hi, I'm Silas, lovely to meet you."

"Peni," he murmured softly, taking Silas's hand and shaking it.

Merihem found himself not liking Peni touching anyone but him, despite the reality that Silas was indeed Dakata's blissful one. He kept his lips tightly shut. "You can let go now," he said a second later when that wasn't happening.

Dakata actually had the nerve to laugh at him. "A blissful one looks good on you, my friend."

"Oh, shut up," Merihem muttered crossly, carefully tucking Peni into his side, not liking the light in Dakata's eyes that suggested he was going to mess with him. "Shall we get back to why we're here?"

"Let's go up to the house, and I'll make us some tea." Silas smiled at them both, slipped his arm through Dakata's, and led him away.

Merihem followed, ever watchful when it became obvious their size difference wouldn't allow him to hold Peni at his side and walk. The house was small but well-equipped and Merihem remembered from his visit to the forest how it sat close to Silas's large oak tree. The branches trailed over the upper part of the structure, connecting them.

Inside they sat, or Merihem did, and placed Peni on his lap when the couch wasn't big enough for them both to squeeze on.

Oh, now please behave because I want none of your nonsense.

What nonsense? I don't know what you're talking about.

Merihem worked very hard to keep his amusement to himself at Peni and his goat's conversation. He was pleased that Peni wasn't upset to be sitting on his lap. That was a real win.

"I think we are going to need a bigger couch if we keep getting visitors." Silas eyed where Peni sat, offering his blissful one a cup. "I don't have milk, but I do have fresh honey to sweeten the tea if you like."

"It's fine, I don't mind black tea." He took the cup and offered a shy smile.

Merihem did his best not to bristle. It was hard.

"So explain what you mean about Mrs. Danials." Dakata, as usual got right to the point.

Peni stiffened, and along came the fretting.

We're gonna be in so much trouble.

Running a gentle, soothing hand up and down Peni's back, Merihem explained, "Mrs. Danials hasn't been cleaning your house, Peni has. She swanned off to Florida on vacation and gave Peni a fraction of what she was earning. Your beautifully clean home was all because of Peni. He was living in the basement because he was homeless, and she totally took advantage of his situation." Once more, he became aggrieved on Peni's behalf.

"I-I w-will pay it all back," Peni croaked.

"You'll do no such—"

"Merihem, let me handle this," Dakata suggested—or demanded, depending on how a person looked at it. "Peni, can I call you that?"

"Of course," he muttered.

Silas stroked a hand over Dakata's casual sweater, smiling at him before handing him a cup. "Have a sip."

He did as he was told, and Merihem felt the tickle of laughter in his throat when Silas came to him and gave him a cup. "Take a drink, it will help relax you."

He was relaxed… wasn't he?

When Dakata gave him a look he was familiar with, 'do it or else', he took a sip. He quirked his brow at Dakata without actually saying, 'happy now', once he took a gulp of the sweet tea. Which actually wasn't half bad for a fruit thing.

"So let me sum up. Mrs. Danials took my money, then gave you a small portion of that money and got you to do her work?" At Peni's nod, Dakata continued on, "Because you had no place to stay, you stayed in my basement with the mice, and she knew this?" Again, another nod.

Dakata swallowed the contents of his cup and rose, slamming it down on the small table close by.

Merihem knew his friend too well, so he tugged Peni closer.

Dakata swung to them and jabbed a finger at Peni. "Pay the money back?" he snarled, and Peni froze like a statue. "Not in this lifetime. Why that convincing bi—"

"Dakata," Silas murmured gently, causing Dakata to come to a stop. Silas rose and glided barefoot to Dakata, slipping an arm around his waist. "Peni does not need anger from you."

"Sorry."

Merihem had never seen his friend look sheepish, and he blinked twice just to make sure he was seeing correctly.

"It's okay, you're angry with me."

Dakata shook his dark head vehemently. "No, not with you. I gave that woman a pay raise because of how clean the house was over the last several months. That was your money, you earned it. She scammed me. I'll make sure it's you who is recompensed."

"I... oh." Peni sagged into Merihem's chest, his hands clutching at Merihem's.

He couldn't resist and kissed the side of his forehead. "See, everything is fine. You have nothing to worry about."

Chapter Fourteen

Peni

It was a relief when Silas suggested he take Peni and show him some of the areas of the forest. Dakata and Merihem were talking business, but Peni had been aware of the dryad watching him. Strangely, neither demon made a fuss when Silas said he was taking Peni for a walk, which was weird, given how Merihem seemed to want to touch him all the time. But Peni was grateful. He seriously needed a minute where he wasn't touching the demon.

"It's very peaceful here. One of my favorite spots, next to my tree, of course." Silas was like a wispy willow, almost gliding across the forest floor.

"I appreciate you showing me." Peni looked around, taking in a huge breath and letting it out slowly.

"One of the reasons I love the forest is that there is such a sense of permanence here." Silas rested his hand on a nearby tree, and Peni could feel a tinge of magic, so different from a demon's, but powerful all the same. "When my mind is jumbled, with too many thoughts competing for space in my head, I can come out here and just breathe."

"I can see where that would be useful. I'm so confused." Peni plopped down on the grass, staring at the tree Silas was stroking.

"A demon will do that to you." Silas gracefully sat on the ground, resting his back against the bark of the tree, his smile gentle. "They are a force of nature, although you have to know Merihem would never hurt you. Demons treat their blissful ones like a shifter's idea of a mate in that regard."

"It wasn't even my idea to claim him." Peni blinked furiously as tears prickled his eyes. "It wasn't that I didn't want to... eventually, but... but..."

Tilting his head to one side, Silas asked cautiously, "Surely Merihem didn't force you…"

"No, it was nothing like that. It was my goat." Peni jumped to his feet, brushing his hands across his eyes, his thoughts spilling out in all directions. "We should've talked. We should've come to an agreement. There are things I never said. Things I don't know, and then Mrs. Danials came in and was beating me around the head with her bag, and then Merihem came and now she's in hell, and my goat claimed my mate. He didn't even ask me—they just did it!"

"You have had a busy morning," Silas said slowly. "I only know a few shifters personally, but it was my understanding that both the animal spirit and the human spirit work in tandem with each other."

"They're supposed to." His sudden burst of energy, combined with the utter chaos of the day so far, had Peni sitting down again. "There are some things people do together that I'm uncomfortable with. That's not Merihem's fault. It's something inside of me that came from…" Peni picked his words carefully. It wasn't as though he knew Silas very well, in fact, barely at all. "…from my time before. Merihem's so confident in everything, absolutely *everything*. It's all so overpowering, and overwhelming, and... I don't know what I'm saying." Peni buried his face in his hands. "I'm sorry. I'll shut up now."

"Don't be sorry, my new friend. If anyone knows how overwhelming demons can be, it's me." Silas's laughter was like a breeze through the trees. "As for shutting up, please don't. I know we've only just met, but I truly want to offer assistance. That's why we're out here. If there's anything I can help you with, even if it's just as someone who can listen to you, then let me do that for you."

"I'm not sure you'll understand." Peni rubbed his hands over his face and looked up. "I don't understand it myself, and that's half the problem. My whole life has just gone boom." He mimed an explosion with his hands. "I didn't have a bad life before Merihem came along. Sure, I was sleeping in a basement which I had no right to do, but Mr. Dakata didn't know I was there until now. I had a routine. Every day I had a specific place in the house to clean—bathrooms one day, kitchen the next. That sort of thing." Even as he was speaking, Peni knew how pathetic that sounded. But Silas was nodding.

"I am much the same with my days," he said. "Every morning at first light I go down to the river, I check the plants, I greet the new growth, and things like that. If I don't get to do that, it's like my whole day feels off and weird."

"Yes. Yes." In that moment, Peni felt as though he'd found a kindred spirit. "There was so much chaos in my life before I got my job at Mr. Dakata's house. I'd been on the streets for so long. But when I was there, I didn't even mind sleeping in the basement. My routine, the cleaning, knowing what I had to do every day and what was expected of me... I felt as if I had some control over me, my life, and who I was. It felt safe to me."

"I can understand that feeling and how important that is. But I have to ask, doesn't Merihem make you feel safe when you're with him?"

"He makes me feel all sorts of things." Peni went to tug at a blade of grass and then thought better of it. Dryads probably frowned on that sort of thing. "I've never had anyone in my life I could trust before. I don't know what that's meant to feel like. I know about mates, and how special they are, but I just feel so rushed..." He trailed off again. "Nothing makes sense right now."

"Tell me then, in an ideal world, what would your mating to Merihem look like? Don't worry about what Merihem wants right now. Think about what your ideal mating is."

"It doesn't really matter, does it?" Peni gave Silas a rueful grin. "If I had my way, we wouldn't even be claimed yet. I know my goat was desperate for the connection—I'm not a complete idiot. It's not like I would ever reject my mate,

I just wanted more time to think about things. If it was up to me, then I'd want answers to questions before I took that step. Like why is Merihem on earth at all? Why do I get the impression he's hiding something from me? Are we always going to live in Mr. Dakata's house, or does he have a house of his own? Who's going to clean that house? Because Merihem doesn't seem to want me doing it at all. My routine's all mucked up and it's only Monday."

Peni's heart started to race, and he got black spots in front of his eyes. "He needs to know about what it was like for me before. Then maybe he'd understand why it'll take time for me to do… to do…" Peni couldn't even say it. "There are some things I'm just not ready for, and while I know my body is giving off one type of signal, that's mating hormones, and I can't help that. He's wandering around with his cock out, looking all sexy and stuff, but I just want to follow my routine today. I'd been with Merihem all weekend. I didn't get five minutes to myself. But instead of scrubbing the kitchen counters today, because Monday is kitchen day, I ended up getting beaten over my head and claiming a demon instead. Why can't anyone understand? I just wanted to clean the kitchen!"

"Hey, hey, hey." Silas was beside him in a blink, his slender arm over Peni's shoulder. "It's okay. Just breathe. Breathe with me. Come on. Inhale, and hold it. Then, let it out slowly… Inhale… softly let it out. You don't have to do anything else in this moment except focus on your breathing."

Peni found himself following Silas's simple advice. In and out. In and out. The first few breaths were definitely shaky, but after a few moments, Peni's heart rate slowed, and he became more aware of the sounds of the forest again.

"I'm sorry. You must think I'm a right wuss."

"There's nothing wussy about getting overwhelmed or showing your feelings." Silas looked up at where the leaves dotted across the sky. "This is a safe space. If you ever feel you need it, then you come here, and you'll always be welcome."

"Thank you." Peni looked around, too. "Just don't ever let me shift out here. My goat will eat anything. I'm surprised he hasn't tried to do it already."

Silas laughed. "That's the circle of life, my friend. Grass and plants grow and get eaten, or sometimes they just wither and die. Your goat is as welcome as you are. But tell me, now you're feeling calmer, what is your gut telling you about your new mate?"

"It's like winning the lottery," Peni admitted. "And I don't mean in a monetary sense. It's like I got what I'd never dared dream I could have. There's just so much. When Merihem was in his demon form over the weekend, we talked. He asked about what I wanted then, and I said I wanted to study to work in a library, and he said I could. Just like that—like it was so easy because he said it could be. But you know, now I know I can, I realize I'll miss him through the day so much if I had to go to classes, because even now, I feel chilled because he's not around."

"There's always online courses," Silas pointed out. "You could do your classes anywhere, even in Merihem's office if he was busy."

"I could." Peni went back to a previous thought, the one that had been nagging at him. "Do you know why Merihem is here on earth living in Mr. Dakata's house?"

"Hmm. I do, and all I can do is promise it's not because of anything bad. Not from an earth perspective." Silas chewed his bottom lip for a second and then added, "You need to hear it from Merihem, though. Sit him down and ask him straight. He will tell you."

"Sit on him, you mean." Peni chuckled. He was quietly glad Silas wasn't the type to betray any confidences. "Merihem seems to be on a mission to keep my butt from sitting in a chair."

"At least you know your butt will never get cold." Silas hugged him again before letting his arm drop down. "And if you can take one more piece of advice, remember that sex between mates or blissful ones is something that happens naturally over time. You don't have to do everything all in one go. You don't ever have to do anything more than you're comfortable with. Being physically close is a natural part of mating, yes, but there are so many different ways that closeness can be enjoyed."

"I don't suppose any of those ways involve me cleaning those kitchen counters."

Chuckling, Silas tilted his head and said, "Whatever rocks your boat, my friend."

Chapter Fifteen

Merihem

He wasn't proud that he'd listened into the conversation between Silas and Peni. But he didn't regret it either. How could he when it helped him to understand his blissful one? Even his demon side didn't have an issue with them doing it.

Merihem had kept quiet the rest of the time as they ate the meal Silas prepared for them. He was mulling over all of his little goat's worries.

Being honest about why he was in the human realm was a start. Also, letting Peni gain back some of the structure to his life, although it wasn't what he wanted for Peni, it was what he needed right now.

All this ran through his mind as the taxicab pulled up.

"Remember, you're welcome here anytime you like," Silas murmured to Peni as he gave him a hug.

Merihem refrained from baring his teeth, that was not what Peni needed or wanted. Dakata didn't hold back the grin that said he knew exactly what was going on in Merihem's head.

They'd managed to fit in talking business in between the spying on Peni. "I'll send over the next contracts to make sure they fit with what you normally do."

Dakata slapped him on the shoulder. "Thanks. But you seem to be doing okay while running around after your blissful one." His toothy smile made Merihem give him a narrow-eyed glare.

He'd shared how things had gone down with Peni when they'd met, including the kick to the balls. His best friend had laughed his ass off.

"You're welcome," Merihem groused, not sounding like he was at all.

"Don't forget to put into place those things we discussed." Dakata gave him a pointed look before glancing at Silas, who was whispering in Peni's ear.

Dakata had a plan for Silas to sing on a big stage in Paris with one of his bands. He was going to be a supporting act and Merihem had gotten tasked with organizing it, so it remained a secret for now from Silas. "Will do."

Silas popped his head in the door of the cab. "Good to see you, George."

"Same," he mumbled around the toothpick.

"Shall we go?" asked Merihem, placing a hand on Peni's waist, stooping to manage it.

He looked at the cab, then at Merihem. "Didn't you want to?"

Merihem chuckled. "Yes."

Another round of goodbyes and they were driving away, this time Peni sat at the side of him, despite Merihem wanting to put him on his lap. He'd heard how Peni found it all too overwhelming and he was trying to turn over a new leaf.

"Did talking with Dakata help with your worries about the money?" Merihem felt that was a good place to start the conversation.

Peni sighed as he wiggled to look at Merihem fully. His brow became pinched. "I'm not sure I'm happy about taking Mr. Dakata's money. I know you told him you already had it in hand. But Mrs. Danials was already paid, which would mean Mr. Dakata has to pay twice. That doesn't seem very fair. I agreed to the rate she offered me. So wouldn't it be wrong to accept more now after agreeing on the terms?"

Merihem resisted scowling at the mention of that woman. Only his blissful one had a point, he had agreed. "What about this..." his mind raced with what he'd heard Peni talk about and a starting point to giving him back his structured life, "You keep on cleaning for Dakata, at the proper rate. That's if it will make you happy. I mean, I want you to do what makes you happy. We could get a new cleaner, and you could supervise them?"—one look at the deepening furrow between his brows and Merihem backtracked—"Or not. It's purely your choice."

Peni gave him a searching look. "You mean that? You wouldn't mind if I cleaned the house?"

Hope, it came through their bond, but also in his voice. Merihem forced a smile. "I want you to be happy." That was complete honesty.

The responding smile, though small, said it was the right thing to say. "I like cleaning."

Merihem recalled the bit about the library science course. "You could maybe do the cleaning in the morning, then maybe if you felt like it, do," he shrugged, trying to act casual, "maybe do an afternoon class for the library stuff. Online or at the college."

Peni tilted his head and back was the searching look. "Were you listening to me and Silas?" he asked suspiciously.

Merihem had no place to shrink in the cab. His lips parted—

"What the... He—"

Peni glanced out the window right at the sound of crunching metal filling the cab, and they spun wickedly fast. Merihem watched as Peni bodily flew into the door, his head ricocheting off the window, which shattered a moment later. His large body, crammed in, hardly moved as he roared, reaching for their blissful one as he slumped down onto the seat unconscious.

What in hell's name? His demon was doing his own roaring as he couldn't emerge as the cab twirled like a ballerina, only with a lot more force as it hit other vehicles. Metal scrapping metal screeched as George wrestled with the steering wheel with bear paws.

Merihem, all set to translocate, found the cab flipping through the air and his head smashed against the roof, then there was nothing but blackness.

"Holy cow, did you see that?"

"The car danced across the Freeway like a puppet on a string."

"Has someone called an ambulance?"

"I did."

Voices floated towards Merihem as his head pounded and something sticky ran down his forehead.

Shake it off. Is Peni okay?

The absolute stark terror coming from his demon side brought Merihem from the haze of pain from his throbbing temple. His arm, though broken, he still clutched at the slight weight he held. He blinked his fuzzy gaze into focus, noting he'd tucked Peni right into his body and except for the wound to his head, he appeared relatively unscathed.

Upside down, he kicked at the battered and caved-in door. His leg protested, but he could already feel his body healing. He kept Peni hugged to his body and got on his back to shuffle out despite the glass shredding his skin. That was of no concern, Peni was all he could think about.

The smell of fuel met his nose as he lay on his back, heaving while looking up at a sea of faces. "Get back," he growled, his demon giving him no time, and emerged to an almighty roar.

His naked body adjusted, the injuries disappearing as those around them scattered like ants at seeing an over seven-foot, naked demon. "Peni. Wake up, Peni," his demon pleaded as they stagger-walked over to a place not scattered with glass and metal to place Peni down on the curb.

I can't feel him through our link.

Shush, let me focus, his demon side demanded. His hands were running over Peni. *He's unconscious. His brain is a little swollen, but he's okay.*

Crackling noises came from behind, along with heat, and distracted them. Glancing back at the cab, flames flickered from the hood. *The bear.*

Our blissful one comes first!

Everyone else scattered because of you. We have to help the bear, too. Merihem felt his demon's reluctance, but he got up and ran to the car, ripped off the caved-in door and lifted a bleeding and unconscious George out of the car to carry him effortlessly to where they'd left Peni. *There,* he snapped, barely stopping short of dropping George to get back to Peni.

Sirens wailed in the distance and Merihem felt his demon gather their magic. There was no way they wanted to have to take their blissful one to a hospital and possibly get separated while they did all sorts of tests that weren't needed. A glow appeared around Peni, seconds ticked by as he willed his demon to heal their blissful one. He didn't care if this brought the wrath of their king, nothing was more important than Peni, not even his own hide.

He'd never have believed he'd feel like this, but all he wanted was Peni back in his arms, whole and safe.

Seconds later, he blinked back his tears, while he and his demon gave an undignified sniff when Peni shifted, and their tiny goat bleated madly at them, hopping about merrily.

"There-there, you're alright." His demon lifted the goat and cuddled him to his dirty chest. "You're safe. We got you."

The ambulance came to a screeching halt, two men jumped out of the front of it, heading in their direction. Then they got a load of his demon and halted.

"He needs help," they growled. "He's bashed his head off the windscreen and the door."

How do you know that?

I didn't pass out!

Chapter Sixteen

Peni

Our demon's in danger. Peni wasn't sure where that thought came from, but he'd never dismiss his goat's instincts. The crash was shocking—Peni had already received one battering that day, and now medical personnel in uniforms were yelling at Merihem, saying he'd gotten knocked unconscious.

You had been. His goat was busy sniffing on either side of Merihem's chest, the big demon refusing to let him go.

You're fine now, you've shifted. We have to get down and sniff around. Our demon is too tall for me to smell anything except him.

I'm not shifting again. I'll be naked in front of all these people. In fact, Peni made a note to have a chat with Merihem's shifting habits. He was sure that with all the powers a demon had, Merihem's demon could wear pants when he shifted. But that was a future issue.

"Sir, I insist. We need to examine the... the... baby goat?"

"He's not a baby, he's a full-grown Pygmy goat." Merihem was still roaring. The crash probably shook up his brain, too.

The goat wiggled and wiggled, and the demon finally bent over and put him down. "Don't go far. I've just got to deal with these idiots thinking they can take you away from me."

Yes, don't get too close to any of the people, Peni warned his animal half. Danger lingered like a giant cloud above the scene and while neither Peni nor his goat could sense where it was coming from exactly, the air was thick with the threat of something.

A huge crowd had gathered, but then that would be because of Merihem as well as the mangled taxicab. How many people could claim they saw a naked demon while on their daily commute? But his goat was tip-tapping his way along the verge, sniffing near George, who was still unconscious and being treated by a medical person.

"Scott's on his way." Of course, Merihem noticed where they were. "I promise he'll take care of the driver and see to his every need." Was he telling Peni or the medic?

I'm so sorry, bear. The goat was sorry, too. It wasn't George's fault they were in an accident. Peni knew that. He'd seen the driver of the vehicle that hit them. He hovered near the unconscious shifter, waiting to see what the medical people would do for poor George.

"We're going to have to give him something quickly before he shifts," someone said, looking at Peni. "Stand back. Something tiny like you would barely make a snack for a shifter this size."

How do they know that about George? More questions. No answers yet.

The goat wandered along, making a point of not looking at anyone in particular, but scanning the crowd.

The driver's not going to be lurking in the crowd. Peni knew that. He would never forget that face. The demon horns, black skin and huge teeth showing from a widely grinning face over the steering wheel would haunt Peni's nightmares.

The demon will have a human form. He will have come back to gloat. Bad guys always do. We just have to scent him. There are too many people here admiring our demon. They should keep their eyes to themselves. The goat showed his teeth and stamped his foot at a young woman who had her phone up, taking a video of Merihem's interactions with the paramedics. *He's ours, not yours.*

We won't know what the demon's human form will look like, Peni protested. The woman jumped back, although Peni noticed she didn't stop pointing her phone. *Merihem and his demon look nothing alike. The demon we saw could be anyone in this crowd. What we need to do is find out why Merihem is here on earth. Maybe he's not supposed to be here. Maybe the demon who crashed into the taxi was someone sent to take the demon away from us.*

They can't. Peni's goat stomped his foot again, causing the woman's partner to move away from them. *He's our mate. Ours.*

I know. I know. Peni froze as he saw a man watching them instead of the scene around the crashed taxi. *Is that…?*

I see him, but that can't be him.

It is. Peni's heart started to race. *It's in the eyes. You can see the demon has the same eyes.*

Nah. The goat danced across the verge a bit and then back again. The man was watching, and then he licked his lips. *He's just a perve with a thing for farm animals. I mean, I can understand it. I'm a prime specimen if there ever was one, but you over there can stop thinking about putting your pencil dick anywhere near my cute fluffy tail.*

Stop that! There were times Peni wished someone would make a bleach that he could use on his brain. *Our mate's in danger. Remember him? That man doesn't want to stick his dick near your behind. He wants to eat us. Look, he's licking his lips again. He's imagining your ribs grilled and covered in gravy.*

The goat snorted. *That man is far too ordinary-looking to be the evil demon. But if you're sure... we can get a bit closer, maybe...*

Maybe we shouldn't. Peni was suddenly worried his goat would do something dangerous, and likely unhelpful. They needed a plan. *Data would need more details. Remember how he works. This is an investigation which means we need to investigate and gather information.*

Hopefully, the goat's fascination with the Android from Star Trek would stop him from doing anything silly. *We need to stay with our mate. We can tell him what we saw, but we need details, answers, you know. All those things I wanted before you claimed him.*

You want to shift back now?

Definitely not. Peni's mental shuddering had the goat's body trembling all over. *Look. George is in the ambulance. He's going to be all right. But that man is working around the crowds and is getting closer. We have to get Merihem to safety. Quick. Faint.*

I am not the type of goat that faints. Indignation ran through their bond.

Move away from the people and closer to our demon, Peni told his goat firmly. *Then, bleat as if you're in distress and faint. Maybe move to the grass verge before you fall over—we've had enough bruises today, but I want you to faint.*

I will not...

Think about it. Merihem will sweep you up into his manly arms, crush you against his heaving chest, and translocate. Get it? He will translocate us to safety.

The goat started moving closer to Merihem, who had worked himself up into a right rage and was now yelling at a policeman. *Can I lick his horns again?*

No, you can't, Peni said hotly, remembering what happened last time his goat did that. *No thinking about sex.*

Think about the answers we need. We have to save our mate.

But then you and he could do sexy body rubbing, yes? The hero always gets the sex when he saves the day.

Let's worry about saving him first, shall we? Peni felt his goat's body slump as the animal fell to his side, letting out a pained bleat. *Good acting skills. Data would've been proud of you.*

Chapter Seventeen

Merihem

With his heart lodged somewhere at the back of his throat, Merihem's demon darted past the police officer and scooped up their blissful one. "Peni. Peni, what's wrong? What happened?" his growl was sinister as the officer approached, appearing like he was about to reach out and touch.

"Do you need the paramedics to come back?"

The goat lifted its head immediately and licked the side of the demon's cheek, heading up towards his horns. The fright turned to something equally unhelpful, but it helped their heart to shift back to where it belonged. "No... no, we're fine. We're leaving," he answered, spying Scott and the driver pulling up.

We need to have a little chat with our goat because something is off.

Off? Our blissful one fainted! Their demon side sounded totally affronted.

No one recovers from a faint like that.

"—can't leave the scene of an accident till I have all the details," the officer blustered, red-faced.

They tuned back in. "Scott, give this officer details of where to find me," he informed the demon, approaching them.

They didn't wait for a reply, and Merihem, for once, was glad for Scott's efficient nature when he pulled out a card as they stalked off.

In the back of the car more suited to his size, Merihem didn't give his demon a chance to do anything, forcing their shift. Holding onto Peni, he stroked a hand over his back. "Can you tell me what that was all about? Did you really faint?" In hindsight, despite what his demon had seen, Merihem wasn't exactly sure the goat had fainted for real.

There were several bleats before Merihem chuckled, and Scott got into the back of the car.

"Where to?" Scott asked, altering the cuff of his suit jacket as he crossed his legs.

"Take us to Dakata's house."

Scott gave the instructions to the driver, and Merihem tried to coax Peni to shift.

By the time they'd got to Dakata's the only conversation he'd had was with a rather giddy goat who'd attempted to climb his chest. Scott had watched them, not revealing any of his thoughts. "I need you to follow up with George, the cab driver. Go to the hospital and pay any bills for his care. See that they look after him."

His blond hair never moved as Scott nodded. "Of course."

Merihem got out of the car, forgetting he was naked, as a woman walked past and gasped. His little goat started bleating and kicking his hooves in the woman's direction when she stopped to stare. Merihem grinned at his possessive little goat's actions. "That told her," he murmured in the goat's ear and got a lick to his face.

He returned his attention to the open door and Scott, hugging his goat closer to him. "I'll not be in the office for the rest of the week. Can you email me everything you want me to look at and courier over anything requiring signing?" He wasn't going to be leaving Peni, he might have healed, but Merihem wasn't taking any chances until he knew what had caused the accident.

"Of course."

A demon of few words, Merihem didn't prolong the conversation when he wanted to find out what was wrong with their blissful one. Something was fishy, and he was more concerned about that than where the driver of the other car who had caused the accident had vanished to.

Inside the house, in his bedroom after translocating, he placed the goat down and turned around, knowing how shy Peni was. "I won't look, so you can shift and get dressed."

There was muttering a second later and Merihem held back his humor.

"Why couldn't I have gotten a less dramatic goat? Why? Did you need to be so…"

"Cute," Merihem supplied helpfully when Peni appeared at a loss.

"He's not cute. And could you please put on some pants? I'm sure when you shift, you could do it wearing pants to stop folks gawking at you, it's not right when you're mi…"

This time he couldn't hold back the chuckle at how peeved Peni sounded at anyone looking at his naked body. "I'll try harder to remember," he answered, doing his best to sound contrite.

He huffed. "That would be a start."

Merihem glanced quickly over his shoulder and caught Peni eyeing his backside with a look that made his cock plump. When their gazes locked, Peni blushed. "Pants. Pants would be good."

As Peni had dressed in the few things he'd deemed to bring from the basement, he turned and in the blink of an eye Merihem had on sweats and a T-shirt. A look from Peni when his gaze traveled down his clothed body showed… *confliction*.

Merihem could work with that.

Then Peni placed his fisted hands on his hips. "I think it's time you and I talked about why you're here."

"Huh?" Changing track, Merihem's head tilted. "Why now?"

"Tell me, please."

Something was most definitely off. Merihem tucked a hand under Peni's elbow. "You need food, and so do I, let me make us something and we can talk while I cook."

"You're going to cook?"

He didn't resist, but he sounded doubtful of Merihem's skills in the kitchen. "Yes, I know you're vegetarian, so I'll make a pasta dish that works for you."

Once in the kitchen and Merihem had helped to seat Peni, getting him a fruit juice, he then went to retrieve every-thing he'd need for a vegetable pasta dish. Taking a mo-ment to wash his hands, he gathered his thoughts. Peni sipped at his juice, watching him closely.

"Silas's sister was taken to the demon realm, kidnapped because of me."

"You?" Peni croaked, spitting out a mouthful of juice.

Merihem nodded and got a cloth to wipe the counter, knowing Peni wouldn't like it messy. "Well, not me exactly, but it might just as well of been. I asked Kisha, another demon, to help Dakata find Silas. It led us all to the forest. Kisha has a big mouth, and he told some other demons about Dakata's blissful connection to a dryad. Only he didn't make it clear that the blissful one was a male, not a female, so evil demons who wanted to hurt Dakata went into the forest and took Wanda."

Out of the corner of his eye, Merihem watched Peni mull that over as he chopped up mushrooms, garlic, onions and egg plant. Before making a tomato sauce. The sounds of bubbling came from the two pans on the stove and broke the silence between them.

"How is that your fault?"

Merihem layered sheets of pasta into the base of a big oven dish. He added the vegetables grated cheese, then the tomato sauce. "I didn't consider how Kisha was."

"So you brought yourself up here as penance?"

"No." Merihem sighed as he picked up the cheese sauce, and poured it over the top layer of pasta. He picked up the packet of grated cheese and sprinkled it liberally over the top of the sauce when he was finished. "I helped Dakata find Wanda, and understandably, he took his vengeance out on those who'd wanted to hurt Silas, and subsequently Wanda. Dakata left a trail of destruction, and the king of our realm wasn't happy."

"Oh…"

"Yep. I should have gone to him. Taken five fucking minutes to clue the king in on the situation as my position deemed, and… things would've been different."

We would've missed out on meeting our blissful one, his demon snarled. But Peni had other things going in that delightful head of his.

"Position? What position is that?"

Merihem turned to look at Peni, who wore a deep frown. "I'm—or was—Controller of the demon realm and the human realm. My role was to deal with those who worked outside the laws by inflicting harm—death on those who didn't deserve it," Merihem explained, thinking he was probably digging himself a grave with how Peni's forehead was a mass of wrinkles.

"So, like a police officer?"

It wasn't technically lying to say yes, but Merihem wasn't going to lie. However, that didn't mean he couldn't take a minute to figure out how to explain what he did without scaring Peni. He placed the dish in the oven and covered it with a lid, setting the temperature. When he couldn't avoid it any longer, he turned to glance at Peni. "In a manner of speaking. Only with greater authority."

"Greater authority?" His brows rose and Merihem could see the cent drop into the slot. "You kill bad people," Peni declared breathlessly.

He nodded. What more was there to say?

Peni shifted on his seat, and Merihem eyed the blush coating Peni's skin. "You aren't put off by that?"

There was more shifting on his seat, before Peni finally shook his head. "You only kill bad people, right?" Once more, Merihem nodded. "Then why would that 'put me off', as you put it? So your penance for helping Dakata and not speaking to your king was being sent up here and losing your job?"

"Yeah. That about sums it up."

"Would what you did be seen as a bad thing by other demons? Black demons, for example?"

About to take a step away from the stove to clean up, Merihem halted. There were only a handful of black demons in their realm. Merihem knew them all, but one in particular, he knew very well. The differing skin color denoted the part of the realm where a demon was born.

His demon growled, and Merihem's stomach twisted into a painful knot at the sense of foreboding that came at Peni seeing a black demon in the first place. "Why are you asking me that?"

Chapter Eighteen

Peni

"Was that the wrong way to describe a demon? Is it impolite to talk about a demon's skin color?" Peni couldn't work out why Merihem's mood changed so quickly. It was almost like the dark cloud they'd sensed back at the crash site, but this time, Peni knew it wasn't directed at him. No one who took the time to make a vegetarian meal for him would kill him before it was cooked. And that's without the mate's angle.

Merihem seemed to guess he'd overreacted as well when, in a gentler tone, he said, "I'm just surprised you've seen another demon. There are other demons in town. You met Scott earlier, and some of Dakata's siblings work at Dakata's company, but I didn't think you'd seen any of them in their shifted form."

"No. Just this other one apart from you." Peni fiddled with his glass.

"Was he wearing pants? Were they a he? Or were your eyes subjected to lady parts?"

Now Merihem was teasing him, Peni could tell. "It was a him, and I couldn't see his bottom half, not in demon form."

"You still haven't said where you saw him. Was he lurking around Dakata and Silas's tree?"

Peni shook his head. "No. Nothing like that. Before I say anything, why did you get upset when I mentioned the black skin? Do you know a demon with black skin?"

"A few of them."

Well, that wasn't helpful. "Are you good friends with a demon with black skin and horns?"

"The only demon I'm good friends with is Dakata, and he doesn't have black skin. Were the horns on the demon black, too?"

"Yes. Why would another demon have a problem with you being with me? How would anyone even know you and I had met?" Peni still felt as though he was only getting half the answers he needed. Merihem was being as evasive again, but Peni wanted some background before he went spouting off what he'd seen.

"Do you remember the lunch you and I enjoyed out together?"

"That was nice." Peni sniffed appreciatively. "But what you have in the oven smells lovely, too."

"Thank you, my blissful one." Merihem's smile changed the whole outlook of his face. "To answer your question, I thought… got an impression, if you can call it that, that someone was watching us."

Peni gasped. "Someone from the demon realm? Why didn't you say something?"

"I got distracted, little one, savoring the fact my blissful one wasn't running from me and was actually sitting within arm's reach." Merihem showed his teeth. "And you are proving to be equally distracting right now, especially when you keep biting that bottom lip of yours. Please tell me when you saw the demon. It's important. I need you to tell me every detail before you forget."

Peni hadn't even realized he was biting his bottom lip. "It's not likely a face I'll ever forget." He looked up at his mate, focusing on the strength he could see in Merihem's eyes. "The demon was driving the truck that hit us. When I looked out of the window. He looked right at me. He was hunched over the steering wheel like this." Peni raised his hands into claws, so they were level with his chin.

"His eyes were black orbs, and I could see all of his teeth. He was laughing like a crazy person. The picture was so clear it was almost as though I could hear the cackling. He didn't stop and wasn't showing any hesitation at all the spilt second before. Then he slammed into the side of the taxi and just disappeared from out of the truck. Well, I think he did because my head hit the window and then it was lights out."

Merihem was watching him so intently, but Peni would've had to have been blind not to notice the tension in his mate's shoulders or the way Merihem was grinding his teeth. "I saw him afterward," he added quickly. "In human form this time. I could tell because of the eyes and the grin. He was in the crowd of people who were watching us." Peni shivered. "I thought he wanted to eat us, but not in the way you look at me sometimes."

"That's why you fainted."

It wasn't a question, but Peni nodded anyway. "I thought, if you believed we were in pain or in danger for any reason, then you'd do your zappy thing and get us out of there. It's not like I could go running up to you with no clothes on. Not with all those people there."

"No one sees you naked except me." Merihem's growl was comforting, letting Peni know some things hadn't changed.

"That's right, and see, that's why we fainted, and that's why we needed for you to get us back here, so I could tell you. But then you told me about Dakata and Silas and what happened when Wanda got taken. All I could think about was if you'd fought that demon then, in the street with all those people..."

"You were trying to protect me, even when you didn't know my story, and yes, you did the right thing." Merihem looked as if he was going to say more. The look between them was so intense, but the timer from the oven went off, and when Merihem turned away, the moment was lost.

The pasta was delicious. Peni particularly liked the way the cheese formed a crusty top, and the vegetables were all cooked just enough to still hold a bit of a crunch. He didn't mind that Merihem didn't seem to want to talk as they ate. He figured his mate had a lot on his mind.

Peni was much the same way. After the story Merihem had told him about how he was effectively under a form of punishment from his king, Peni was determined that before Merihem did anything against the demon with the maniacal laugh, he would have to get permission from his king first. It wouldn't be what Peni would do. It definitely wasn't anything any shifter would do, especially when it came to protecting a mate, but Peni was going to make sure that Merihem didn't get himself into any more trouble than he was already in.

"That was truly delicious, thank you." Peni pushed aside his empty plate with a grateful sigh. "My belly is completely full. You're an amazing cook."

Merihem was pleased. It showed in his smile, and the warmth of his eyes.

"I'll get up and do the dishes in a minute," Peni promised. "I just want to take a moment and enjoy this food settling in my gut."

"This house has a dishwasher," Merihem reminded him. Peni knew that, but he'd never used it. Then Merihem added, "You should know, I heard a lot of what you told Silas earlier today, when you and he went for your walk."

"You heard all that?" Peni wanted to sink under the table. "Did Dakata hear about it, too?" *Oh, my gods, if he did, then I'm never visiting the forest again.*

Merihem shook his head. "No. Dakata was focusing on what his blissful one was saying, the same way I was focusing on you. It's not like we've got supersonic hearing. We were eavesdropping so I could check in on you, mentally. You know to make sure you were comfortable being out with someone you'd just met."

"That's why you didn't kick up a fuss when Silas suggested we go out for a walk. You already knew you could monitor me from afar." Peni rubbed his hands over his face. *I have to face this.* He looked Merihem in the eyes. "Well, now you know what a mess I am. You're this virile studly demon, and you got stuck with a nervous… a nervous goat. And what does it say about me when my goat is more sexually adventurous than I am?"

"You have issues." Merihem shrugged. "I can't confess to knowing what that feels like, but that doesn't mean I'm going to laugh at you for it. Except I have to know this. It's important for us going forward. Has anyone physically or sexually abused you?"

"Only my eyes and my ears, and when I think about it, my nose having to smell all that…" Peni shuddered. "I grew up in a household where sex was something my father did every single day. He never cared who saw him. He and his many partners would go at it in the living room, in the kitchen. No surface was ever clean. And when I got older, he thought I'd join in. Him and his friends, male and female. They used to laugh at me when I just wanted to hide in my room."

Looking down at the clean counter, Peni ran his finger across it. "That's why I enjoy working here. It's quiet, peaceful and clean. Mr. Dakata never brought partners home, he was barely ever here."

"But that's not the only reason you're not a fan of sex, though, is it? Because it dirties up the countertops."

"And the living room couches, chairs, the dining room table—my dad's spunk was everywhere. I had to go outside just to get away from the smell." Peni sighed and then said in a quiet voice. "No, that's not all that bothered me. It was the acts themselves. Everything I saw. No one seemed to care about each other. It was all rough, with a lot of yelling, and shoving, and slapping skin, and hair pulling. My dad's partners seemed to enjoy it. They were always laughing afterward. But none of them cared about each other—not my father, his friends, or the people they were playing with. Surely, if someone wants to get naked with someone else, then shouldn't they care about each other first?"

"I'm probably not the right person to ask. I like being naked because I can't stand how clothes feel on my skin. Cloth chaffs my bits and makes me feel restricted, and that's in either form."

"That's not going to get you out of wearing pants when we're out of the house." Peni shook his finger at his mate. "Get some harem pants or something similar, so your balls bob about with gay abandon if you have to. But if people can't see me naked, then they can't see you with no clothes on either."

"I will do my best to remember." Reaching across, Meri-hem took his hand. "I'm also not the best person to talk to when it comes to caring for the people I've had sex with in the past, but I know I care deeply about you already. What I know is that there are so many ways two people who do care for each other can get off with each other—it can be a truly pleasurable experience with none of the penetration or hair pulling that you witnessed."

Frowning, Peni asked. "You mean you don't want to penetrate me?" *Perhaps I have gotten this all wrong.* Except no. Merihem was shaking his head.

"I want that, yes. More than you could ever know. But it would be no fun for me if you weren't ready, if you were doing something because you thought you had to, just to make me happy. The thing is we could start small, get used to being naked together and find a way that brings us both an orgasm without anything too intrusive. It could be on a bed… or the kitchen counter, if you prefer."

"Not the counter." Peni shook his head wildly. "I just mentioned that to Silas because I would relax better if it were clean before, you know, we did anything else."

"I can arrange that." Grinning widely, Merihem got up and stacked the dishes they'd used all along one arm and took them over to the kitchen bench. "Can I just stack them in the sink for now, or do I have to rinse them and put them in the dishwasher?"

It was in that moment that Peni lost his heart to his demon. No one had ever wanted to clean for him before. While he knew he wasn't ready for the heavy sex stuff he'd seen growing up, Merihem was really easy to look at naked. *I hope he thinks the same about me,* Peni thought as he said boldly, "I'll do the dishes later. I'm not promising anything, but maybe as it's getting late, we could try this bed stuff."

Chapter Nineteen

Merihem

The urge to jump up and fist pump the air at those few little words that made everything inside Merihem fire with passion was hard to resist. Instead, he nodded like a gentleman would and finished what he was doing.

He wiped his hands on a cloth, laid it on the sink in the right place, and walked over to Peni. He eyed his courageous goat and slipped his arms around him to lift him off the seat. Eyeball to eyeball, he made a promise. "I'll do whatever you want and stop the second you say no." His nose wrinkled, and Merihem kissed the tip. "I promise. If it isn't working for you, just say so. I won't be mad or upset."

Peni searched his gaze. "You mean it?"

"Absolutely."

Peni hesitated, then his arms crept around Merihem's neck, and his demon swooned at how he played with the hair at the nape of their neck. "Okay." His fingers clung a little tighter. "Can you zap off my clothes? I don't think my fingers are up to the job with how shaky I feel."

"We can stop right now, go to bed and sleep. It's been a long ass day." He hadn't finished speaking when Peni blushed and shook his head.

"I want to try."

Those four words made Merihem's cock ready to bust through his sweats. *Slow. We have to take it slow.*

Merihem could have translocated them to the bedroom, but he wanted to give them both the time to let the reality of what was coming next sink in. For him, it was all about reacting to what made Peni feel good. For his blissful one, the need to be assured nothing would happen he didn't want.

In the bedroom, Merihem went to turn on the lamps, not putting Peni down when he could feel his body reacting to their closeness. There, he decided he wanted something a little more romantic. A quick incantation and candles floated about the room. Flames flickered as they danced around the bed. He also added in a protection element, so they didn't get caught unawares—literally with their pants down.

Peni's eyes widened, and his heart rate picked up as he got dreamy-eyed. Merihem added some scent to the candles to reduce the smell of cum—hoping they both would—recalling what had been Peni's past experience.

And with a flourish, he conjured a velvet throw for the bed that would feel nice against his blissful one's naked skin. Peni gave him a shy smile that struck right at the center of Merihem's being. He came closer as he removed their clothes with a thought and kissed Peni softly.

His lips glided gently over Peni's, learning the contour of his mouth. Nibbling on his full lower lip until it trembled and parted. The sigh that followed encouraged Merihem to linger. To sip at Peni like he was a fine wine. Attuned to every sound he made, Merihem wanted to ensure they kept their promise.

The fingers in his hair tightened as his warm, naked skin pressed closer. His desire grew along with Peni's as he trailed his lips over his jaw and down the side of his throat, teasing the flesh. He nipped it gently when Peni made a whining noise in the back of his throat before gasping, his shaft slicking up Merihem's stomach as he rocked his hips in a slow grind, almost as if unaware of what he was doing.

Merihem did.

Fuck, did he.

His blissful one's scent was intoxicating as their body warmth and Peni's rocking caused the aroma to rise between them. Merihem trailed kisses over Peni's collarbone and arched him back so he could reach his nipples. He flicked his tongue over the bud, and Peni melted in his arms, his lips parted, wearing a look of awe.

This was what he wanted. As reluctant as he was to put Peni on the bed, Merihem realized that to get to both nipples easily and him not to be bent in two, it was the best option. He sucked the pink bud between his lips and teased the tip with his tongue as he placed Peni on the velvet cover.

An erotic groan from Peni left Merihem struggling not to come all over his blissful one. His cock throbbed painfully, and his balls hugged his body while his spine tingled. He willed his body to behave as he continued to tease Peni's nipples.

"Ohhh, my… ohhh, please."

Merihem moved from one to the other, then used his fingers to tease the wet nubs directed by Peni's continuous stream of sexy sounds. Peni pushed up into each touch, enhancing the experience for Merihem. Never had he felt the joy of taking pleasure from his partner in this way. Merihem became convinced he would come untouched just from listening to Peni's sounds and touching him like he was.

When Peni's hips kept up a rhythmic motion of thrusting up, Merihem eased back to kneel beside him. His heavy-lidded eyes did a number on Merihem as he stroked fingers over the quivering belly towards Peni's pretty, slim cock. Pink and flushed, the head was slick with pre-cum that Merihem wanted to taste.

He ran a fingertip over the slippery flesh, swirling the pad of his finger in the sticky cum, noting all of Peni's reactions. When he lifted it, inhaling, his gaze remained on Peni as he slowly sucked his finger into his mouth, an elicit moan pouring from between his lips. Peni's eyes tracked the move. His skin was flushed and dewy.

"Fuck, you taste so delicious."

A deep rose color spread up his chest as his eyelids dipped. "Do I?"

The breathy question was Merihem's undoing. He stretched out his body next to Peni's until his groin was easily accessible. Peni's gaze was back on Merihem as he stroked a finger down the velvety skin before lifting and angling the cock for him to better reach it with his tongue. With a feverish stare encouraging Merihem, he teased them both by running the flat of his tongue over it, barely touching.

"Ohhhh…"

Eyelids fluttering, Peni's lips were back to parted as his hips moved up to push the cock closer to Merihem's tongue in invitation. *He likes it.*

Thank fuck, he likes it.

Swirling his tongue over the spongy head, his eyes remained on Peni the whole time. The slim hips juddered, and the shaft slipped a little further between Merihem's lips. Taking the hint that Peni wanted more, he sucked him deeper. The scent and flavor were a heady combination. He licked down the underside of the pulsing flesh till he reached Peni's balls, then lapped at them, his tongue slipping under to get a cheeky swipe at Peni's hole.

"Oh… Oh… Oh… wowwwww," he cried out, and Merihem drew back unsure if he'd gone too far, to watch Peni's slender body arch, his eyes close, a beautiful flush covering his body as he came apart. Ribbons of cum landed on his stomach and chest before Merihem could wrap his lips around Peni's cock and drink down the rest of his release.

By the time he'd sucked him dry, Merihem was in pain, hanging on the precipice, but not quite able to come despite how aroused he was.

He rolled onto his back, chugging in big breaths to calm his own ass down when Peni's whole body went lax. "That... that was..." Peni couldn't seem to find his words.

Merihem grinned up at the ceiling, regardless of whether he hadn't had a release. At Peni's loss for words, Merihem would take that as he'd rocked the entire experience for his blissful one.

The mattress moved next to him and Merihem turned his head to look at his blissful one. A hand ran over his belly, causing it to quiver.

Peni's gaze traveled down to where Merihem's cock lay heavy against his stomach, and back was the shy goat. "Can I touch it?"

Throat drier than if he'd taken a visit to hell, Merihem could only nod. Expecting Peni to stroke it with his fingers that were dancing over his stomach, his jaw dropped at how Peni scooted down the bed and then leaned over

Merihem's dick, eyeing it so intently that Merihem's skin burned.

"You don't ha…" Merihem bit his lower lip to hold back the unmanly squeal that came at the tentative tongue licking at the enormous head of his shaft. Peni's fingers hardly reached halfway around his girth when he took hold of the middle of his cock.

It looked enormous in Peni's hand, and he held perfectly still, not wanting to frighten his blissful one. Peni took a deep breath, then a hot, moist breath bathed his cock before Peni's mouth widened, and a pink tongue poked out to lap at him gently.

Releasing a deep guttural moan at the move, Merihem panted, sweating at the effort to hold back.

"That okay?" Peni questioned, almost against the sensitive skin torturing Merihem inadvertently.

"Hummmm," he grunted. *Don't move. Don't move. Holy fuckkkkkk!*

Peni's mouth stretched wider, and he wiggled his jaw as his lips enclosed just the head of Merihem's cock. Then he swirled his tongue over the slit.

Merihem's body shook while his eyes rolled into the back of his head as he deflated so fast when the air left his lungs at force. Sensations blew the top of his head clear off at the tentative playing with his dick. As blow jobs went, it was awkward and sloppy. It was the best fucking blow job of Merihem's life. As Peni swallowed and lapped at his slit, groaning, the vibration hit his balls and he bellowed, muscles seizing as his balls unloaded.

Cum dripped out the corners of Peni's mouth, but he didn't pull back, and he continued to make sounds that were all delight.

Minutes later, sweat-soaked and panting harder than a racehorse at allowing Peni to keep it at his pace, his blissful one sat back. He used the back of his hand to wipe his chin, and there was the shy smile. "How was that?"

Merihem's lips curled up into a huge grin. "When I get my brain cells to work again, I'll let you know."

Peni's brows drew together, then a second later smoothed out. "That's good, right?"

"Any better, and I might never want to leave this bedroom."

The sweet giggle seemed at odds with what they'd just done as Peni rested his head on Merihem's stomach. Merihem relaxed and enjoyed the simple pleasure of being close in this way. As time passed, he thought Peni had fallen asleep, drifting himself. His eyelids fired open when

Peni whispered, "I liked it. I think next time I'd like to try something else, if that's alright?"

Merihem released a shuddery breath at there being a next time and stroked a hand over Peni's hair, pushing it back to look at him. "Of course," he murmured. "Do you have something in mind?"

Peni nosed into his side, hiding his face. "Licking other... places."

Oh, to the demon gods!

Chapter Twenty

Peni

"We're going to speak to the king now?" Peni was still sorting his new experiences into fresh boxes he'd had to make in his brain. They were still in the bedroom, although Peni had thrown his clothes back on the moment they'd woken, and Merihem had cleaned them up. But then he remembered what he'd vowed to himself before Merihem had totally melted his brain. "I mean, yes, of course, we should go now. I don't want you getting into any more trouble with your king. Should I shower first?"

Merihem shook his head. "There is no shame in that we smell of each other. It will reinforce to the king the strength of our bond," he said, his voice deepening. "Unless the smell is offensive to your precious nostrils."

"No. Not offensive." *Just really strong.* Peni didn't think he'd ever smelled so intensely of anything other than himself before. He knew he hadn't. His goat half was snickering in his head, thrilled that his human half was overcoming his *limitations*, as his goat called it, and now Peni was going to have to meet a Demon King, smelling... unlike himself. "I can do this, and yes, we will go. What do I wear to meet a king? Is there a protocol for that sort of thing?" He looked down at his worn pants and t-shirt. "Should I have a button-up shirt? I could go and buy one..."

He felt the tingle of Merihem's magic sweeping over him and gasped, his hands running over the new material. "You got me a new coat. It's beautiful."

"It's a vegan leather." Merihem grinned. "I know these things are important to you."

"It is, thank you." Peni rubbed over his arms, hugging itself. "But, you know, will I even need a coat? Isn't it hot where we're going?" He peered up at his mate, hoping he wasn't suggesting anything offensive.

"We're not going to hell." Merihem burst out laughing, slapping his still naked thigh, half bent over with glee. "Oh, for fuck's sake. Is that what you thought, little one? That I lived in hell? That I would subject my precious blissful one to fire and brimstone and the screams of the damned?"

Horns. Unusual colored skin. Claws and fangs. "I wasn't sure. I've never been to another realm before." Peni went back to examining his new coat. The dark brown material was soft under his fingers. The coat went all the way down to his knees, and it had two big pockets, one on each side. "But for future reference, it sounds like you know that place, and shifter ears are very susceptible to extremely loud noises like screaming."

"I would never take you anywhere that would cause you any discomfort," Merihem promised as he held out his hand. "Ready to go?"

Peni looked at the hand, and then down at Merihem's naked... legs. Yes, it was the legs. Nothing else to see, nope, nope, nope. Peni wasn't going to get distracted. He was just looking at the legs. He waited. His mate was intuitive.

"Peni? Peni. Did you have more questions?" Nope, not intuitive. Confused.

Tapping his toe on the soft rug under his foot, which didn't make the necessary noise he needed, Peni sighed instead. If his eyes were lasers, Merihem's legs would have holes in them.

"What are you looking at?" Merihem looked down in the same direction as Peni's gaze. "Did I miss a bit of cum? No. I got it all. What's wrong with my legs?"

"Really? What's wrong with them?" Peni glared at his mate's face. "I can see them." He waited, but Merihem was still looking at him with that sweet, confused expression that only a ruggedly handsome man could give. "If I can see your legs, then other people can see your legs."

"I'm going to be in demon form when I speak to the king," Merihem said slowly.

"And your demon form is going to be wearing pants when he stands in front of other people who have eyes, I assume?"

Peni could see the "no" hovering on Merihem's tongue, but then his mate straightened and sighed. "It will likely be unbearably uncomfortable, but my demon will wear pants while we're out. Just for you," he added, clearly thinking Peni wouldn't get the point.

"Thank you. You do that, and then we'll go." Time for a smile. Merihem didn't need to know Peni was terrified of meeting a royal person—a royal demon. Nope. If his demon could overcome the habits of a lifetime and wear pants, Peni could bury his fear and meet the personage with his head held high.

The demon realm wasn't what Peni expected. For one thing, he was glad Merihem had magicked him up a coat. Looking around the bleak hall, with its super high ceilings and the tall columns made of gray stone—a color theme—that was everywhere Peni looked. "Is this a castle?"

"It is Asmodeus's waiting room. I suppose you would call it a castle on the earth realm." Merihem was in his demon form, and Peni had to bend his neck back even further than usual to see his demon's face.

"They don't believe in chairs?" Peni dropped the demon's finger he'd been holding and turned in a full circle. There wasn't a single table or chair anywhere. There also weren't any pictures or windows. Just stone as far as the eye could see. Everything felt big, gray, and harsh. The only break in the stone walls and columns was a set of giant black curved doors that were covered in elaborate carvings depicting scenes Peni didn't want to examine too closely. They reminded him of activities he'd gotten forced to see when he lived at home.

"Our king doesn't like for his demons to think this is a place they can just hang out and spend time in. He values his privacy and only sees demons for important matters."

"Were we meant to make an appointment?" Peni couldn't hear anything except his own heartbeat.

"Asmodeus knows we're here." The demon's chuckle was so much deeper than Merihem's, but Peni felt there was a touch of nervousness there as well. He curled his hand around Merihem's finger again, giving it a comforting squeeze.

"Is there…" A bleat fell out unbidden as the huge doors slammed open. The demon standing there filled the doorway—he was that big. His horns were longer than Merihem's, his shoulders wider, his legs stronger, and yes, Asmodeus was wearing pants. But the lighting glistened on the demon's chest muscles, causing them to shimmer like Peni imagined dragon skin might do.

"Merihem and personage. Interesting. Enter."

A demon of few words. Peni could appreciate that. He bit his own tongue, not wanting to suddenly start rambling—something he was prone to do when he was nervous. Everything about Asmodeus was intimidating.

As he strode across the floor, Peni noticed the bigger demon was graceful. There was no lumbering in those strides. Asmodeus turned and sat on a golden throne that had deep red cushions, likely there to stop the royal butt from falling asleep during meetings.

"Sit." He waved a finger at a couple of chairs that suddenly appeared in front of the stage the throne was on.

"Many thanks, sir." Merihem's demon bowed his head, and then a large hand ushered Peni towards the seats. Peni perched himself on the edge of the hard wood—no cushions for visitors, he noticed, although Merihem remained standing.

"Sir, Gebre has caused grievance against my blissful one, and I have come to seek permission to deal with him in accordance with our laws."

The words were strong and respectful, but rather than ask questions or anything, which Peni thought a king might do, Asmodeus chuckled.

"You are that intent on your vengeance, you don't think to introduce me to the person by your side first?"

Merihem clearly wasn't expecting that. "Sir, my apologies. I did not wish to waste any of your valuable time. This is Peni, a pygmy goat shifter and my blissful one. We have claimed each other."

"I'm aware." Asmodeus got up, came down the steps, and knelt in front of Peni's chair, studying him intently. Up close, the man's power was overpowering, yet Peni didn't feel there was any threat coming from the demon. *At least my goats claimed now and not trying to lick those horns.* Although his cheeks flushed as Asmodeus chuckled again. *My gods, can he read my thoughts?*

"How did you and my demon meet, little one?"

Glancing up at Merihem's demon—his demon wasn't showing any emotion—Peni looked back at the king. "I was cleaning Mr. Dakata's house, Your Kingship, and Merihem came to stay. He chased me around the kitchen and my goat told me we were mates."

"Ah, yes. Something I learned recently. Shifters refer to their blissful ones as mates, don't they?"

Peni nodded. It was difficult to meet Asmodeus's eyes. "Merihem explained the words might be different, but the bonds are the same."

"And Gebre threatened those bonds?"

How much do you already know? "I saw a demon driving a truck that crashed into the taxicab Merihem and I were in. The crash was intentional. I blacked out for a short while. The driver, a bear shifter, is still in hospital I think. I didn't want to say anything to Merihem at the time because I didn't want him to get into trouble on earth. But I described the demon to Merihem when we got back to Mr. Dakata's house, and he determined it had to be the one you mentioned. Unless that demon has a twin?"

Straightening up, Asmodeus shook his head. "No. Gebre has no twin, and those are the actions I would expect of someone who let a recent promotion go to his head and will do anything to hang onto it. But in the spirit of the same fairness you endeavor to show, we will confirm the identification first."

There was a tug in the air. Peni felt it and just as he was looking around, wondering what was going on, another demon appeared at the side of them.

That face!

Peni gasped and shrank back against Merihem's leg, and his demon snarled.

"Sir." The demon bowed low and kept his head down. "Is there a problem here? Did you need me to take *care of these two* for some reason in my position as Controller?" The words dripped with disdain.

"Idiot." Asmodeus sneered. "As if I couldn't do that myself if that were my intention. Look up, worm. Show your face."

"I'm showing respect for your position, my king." Gebre wasn't looking up. "After being granted such an auspicious promotion to such an important position in your realm, I would never overstep—"

"Shut up. Look up. Look at me!" Asmodeus's roar bounced off the walls. Peni wanted to cover his ears, it was so loud, but it stopped quickly.

"Answer me, little one." Asmodeus had gentled his voice. "Is this the face you saw?"

Nodding, Peni remembered it was probably respectful to use his words. "Yes, Your Kingship. That is the person who caused the car crash that could've killed me, and severely injured our bear shifter driver."

"That's all I need." Peni got zapped out of his chair, and suddenly he was sitting on Asmodeus's arm like a parrot. "Gebre, you're fired. Merihem, permission granted to avenge your blissful one and resume your controller position. Sentence to be carried out immediately."

Merihem looked conflicted. "Thank you, sir. What about Peni? He shouldn't see…"

"You're absolutely right, Merihem, and I am pleased my reinstated Controller has such respect for his blissful one's feelings. I will look after him. You can come and find us when you're done."

"Sir?"

But Peni heard nothing else because Asmodeus just zapped them away into yet another room. This one was comfy, with big couches, soft rugs on the floor, and a fire blazing in an oversized fireplace.

"Don't be nervous. Take your coat off, have a seat, and get comfortable. Would you like refreshments?" A large silver tray appeared on a solid wooden coffee table.

"If you had some juice, that would be lovely, thank you." Peni took off his coat and laid it on the seat beside him. "This is very kind of you," he added.

"Not what you expected, I'm sure." Asmodeus did have a lovely smile. "Merihem has a messy job to do, and I'm curious about blissful ones. They are very rare, and we have few records of them in our archives. I would love to hear about your experiences with my demon so far. Do you mind?"

Probably better than watching Merihem tear Gebre's head off his shoulders. "What would you like to know? We've not been together very long, but I'm happy to share anything I know."

Chapter Twenty-One

Merihem

Conflicted by thoughts of what Asmodeus was doing with his blissful one, by getting reinstated, and what that would mean to his bond with Peni, Merihem had to work to gain focus when the king disappeared holding Peni. He had no quarrel with the king, but still, he itched to follow them and make sure Asmodeus put Peni down and kept his hands to himself.

He and his demon didn't like to be separated from their blissful one in their realm regardless that Peni was with their king.

Would he protect Peni if someone were to attack?

Do you need to be having thoughts like that? his demon demanded as Gebre snarled at them.

They eyed the large, black demon wearing an ugly sneer, who had never been a favorite with them. Gebre had proved with his actions that he had no regard for the lives of others. He killed for the pleasure of it, and that made him dangerous to both worlds. A killing demon was not what being Controller was all about. It was about balance, about protecting both worlds from wrongdoers.

"Why?" Merihem asked out of interest. He'd never done anything to Gebre. He'd had no quarrel with him other than he'd never liked the other demon.

"You are in the way of what I want." He shrugged his massive shoulders, his eyes going sly. "Asmodeus would have eventually seen you for what you are." He stepped closer, his teeth revealed in a snarl. "Weak."

Merihem laughed heartily at that. "Weak?" He shook his head, working to hold on to the next bout of laughter. "Weak is using my blissful bond against me. Of believing that it would make me weak." This time it was Merihem's turn to snarl, his teeth gleaming as he gritted out, "Peni strengthens me in every way. That is your failure. You never learned to see beyond your own needs."

The sound Gebre made prepared Merihem for what was coming. Gebre, he'd trained. He understood what pushed the other demon's buttons. Merihem had been right all along—Gebre was indeed the wrong demon to be Controller.

Merihem went into a battle stance, one he had taught the fuckwit standing looking way too fucking smug at the move. He would not use his power here to slay Gebre, they wanted to beat the life right out of the poor excuse of a demon. Nothing else would do after what he did to Peni, harming him. "You failed. It appears I'm not a skilled teacher when it comes with a dose of 'asshole' attached to the demon. But that's okay, because now I'm gonna show you exactly how fucking skilled I really am at causing pain."

Merihem anticipated the frontal attack because Gebre was that predictable. The demon had learned nothing, it seemed. Merihem easily dodged Gebre, who had to skid to a stop to avoid plowing into the stone wall. Goading him, Merihem laughed. "You were never light on your feet either, were you?"

"Fucker," Gebre screamed. "You will die by my hand, and Asmodeus will see I am the better demon!" He lunged once more, the wicked-looking claws striking out.

They hit the air as Merihem danced around the other demon. He could easily rip out the fucker's throat, but that would be too easy and over far too quickly. They wanted to make him suffer first.

Merihem let Gebre get closer the next time and pivot turned, kicking out and landing a heavy blow to Gebre's midriff. He staggered, but only for a second, just long enough for Merihem to run his claws down the other demon's arm, tearing the black flesh down to the bone.

His scream was music to Merihem's ears. "Having fun yet?" he taunted.

Gebre spun and kicked back, only to miss and roar, this time in frustration.

Merihem laughed gleefully when the air around Gebre shimmered, but then nothing happened. Asmodeus had clearly expected Gebre to fight dirty and attempt to use his powers. "Oops, did you lose something?" he sneered, before lunging and slicing across Gebre's chest, flaying the skin and muscles.

The scent of blood filled the air as Gebre lost all control, screaming and spitting as he launched himself at Merihem, who easily dodged. Blood oozed, gleaming dark red against Gebre's skin as he landed one solid punch to the side of Merihem's arm. It hurt, but it was nothing more than an irritation.

Merihem danced around the flailing demon, striking, slashing, and tearing flesh from Gebre's bones because he could, and without the use of his power. He would never disgrace himself in that way.

When Gebre went to his knees bellowing in pain, Merihem grabbed his hair, wrenching back his head. He looked Gebre right in the eye as he ripped out his throat, silencing him. "Take that, you motherfucker asshole, for harming what is most precious to us. May your soul sit in the never lands, to be fed on by the undead for all eternity." Gebre disappeared as he uttered the last words, using his power to rid the realm of the shit.

Chest billowing, Merihem stared at the mess on the floor and sighed. Cleanup was a bitch and a necessity if he didn't want to upset Peni. His little pygmy goat was really rubbing off on him. He chuckled at the notion. Did it hurt to hope for that later as a reward?

Minutes later, the place was restored to how it looked before the incident. Merihem eyed himself, releasing another sigh at the state of himself. The pants that Peni insisted upon were stuck to his skin, rubbing in uncomfortable places. The time it took to get cleaned—properly—and go in search of Asmodeus left Merihem anxious like he hadn't been when fighting with Gebre. What had they been talking about?

Maybe playing with Gebre had been the wrong thing, now he came to think about it, with how nervous Peni got. Asmodeus was not the most civil of demons.

He followed Peni's scent, and at the king's personal chamber, Merihem's anxiety spiked. He knocked, waiting to be granted entrance. Seconds ticked by.

Could he hear laughter beyond the door?

He knocked again, harder.

The door swung open and Merihem had to resist snarling at Asmodeus, who chose to sit very close to Peni, grinning at him in such a way, Merihem's eyes widened.

The man looked human.

"Come in, your Peni is a delight," he announced, like it was normal for him to say such things.

Only Merihem couldn't get his feet to move at the shock of such a statement coming from the king of the demon realm.

"Stop standing there looking like I've hit you," he growled and set Merihem's world back into its rightful place.

"Sorry, yes, sir." Merihem came into the room and noticed none of his surroundings, his full interest was on Peni.

Are you okay?

Peni started and then gave him that shy smile that went straight to a part of his anatomy that loved it. *Yes. Your king has lots of questions.* Peni's gaze swept over his as his brows drew together. *Is that a bruise on your arm?*

The one blow Gebre had landed was more like a bee trying to sting his thick demon skin. *I'm fine.* He hadn't noticed it, or he would have healed it.

Peni was up and off the seat, stomping towards him. His gaze narrowed on Merihem's body. *Oh, my.* His cock plumped, and he tried to get his thoughts to go someplace else.

"Let me see for myself." Gentle fingers ran over his arm as Peni strained to reach the spot where Gebre had hit him.

In the end, Merihem got down on his knees, ignoring his king while Peni fussed over him, making a tutting noise. "That big bully."

"I dealt with him." He locked away anything that would clue Peni in to exactly how that had happened.

"Good." Peni sniffed, and Merihem rose, picked him up, and tucked him into the crook of one arm.

Peni rested his cheek against his shoulder.

Asmodeus met Merihem's gaze over Peni's head. "Sir, I know we need to discuss the position of Controller—"

"Discuss…" one brow arched up, and Merihem resisted squirming. "What would we need to discuss?"

Tell him. His demon was very pushy. "Peni would not be comfortable living in this realm, and I wouldn't feel happy leaving him here while I was… working."

"I see."

Did he? Merihem wasn't so sure. But he was picking up Peni's relief at the conversation, so he pushed on. "I could reside in the human realm, like I did here. It would make no difference to my ability to carry out my role." No, that would happen when he had to leave his little goat.

As if Asmodeus read his thought his smooth brow furrowed. "You could," he suggested, his gaze on Peni. "Your blissful one could keep me company while you are *busy*. He will be safe with me."

Merihem wasn't so sure of that, although Peni was showing no signs of distress at the suggestion. What had they talked about?

"Thank you for the offer. I'll give it some thought after I have discussed it with Peni. Ultimately, it would be his decision."

Asmodeus didn't hide his surprise. "Unusual," he murmured, then nodded. "Fine. Now you may take your leave."

And just like that, they were back in Dakata's house. Peni snuggled a little closer and Merihem's demon receded. "He's a nice man—Demon King—I think he's lonely."

Chapter Twenty-Two

Peni

In honesty, Peni's brain was a little muddled, and it wasn't any clearer after a long week with Merihem checking over every inch of his body every night and half the day to make sure he was all right after being in the demon realm. Peni still got to clean the house while Merihem worked at Dakata's office, but the demon realm sat like an elephant in the living room and wasn't budging.

The demon realm was a place Peni didn't like. That was something he could share with Merihem, and he did a couple of times when Merihem stopped kissing him long enough so they could talk. He hadn't seen a single plant down there. The atmosphere was full of tension. Peni enjoyed his time with Asmodeus, although... their conversation had confusing bits, too, and Peni wasn't sure he should even mention any of that.

Not that Merihem seemed keen on being reminded Peni had spent time alone with another man anyway, so he wasn't pushing for details. It was almost a relief when Merihem cleared his throat after breakfast a week later and said, "Would you be all right in the forest for a few hours this morning? You could spend time with Silas, I know he'd be pleased to see you. If you're with him, then I can trust Dakata will look out for you, too."

"I don't mind." Peni looked up from his plate, hoping his relief wasn't showing. "I appreciate you understanding I'm not keen on visiting down there. You know, so soon after last time. Being in the forest would be lovely. Maybe I could let my goat out for a bit, if Silas doesn't mind."

"I'm not keen on leaving you alone for any length of time at all, but I want to get things organized for us going forward." Merihem leaned his elbows on the table, looking serious, and Peni realized he was expected to pay attention. "I know you enjoy the cleaning here, so I'm going to speak to Dakata about buying this house. That way, your cute little animal side can have fun in the garden out the back here, with me keeping an eye on you, of course. But you could do that every day if you wanted to. We can always buy more plants."

"That sounds wonderful." Peni clapped and grinned. "I used to look out of the window in the basement in the evenings sometimes, watching the trees blowing in the breeze. My goat was always longing to go and play in the bushes out there. But I was always afraid he would eat too much, and we'd be found out."

"I'll make that happen for you." Merihem used that tone that always made Peni feel special, and he blushed. "But I also need to speak to the king about my job as Controller."

That made Peni pause for a moment. "That is really important, isn't it? Do you have to kill people every day? Only, I'm thinking if you do, then you might need to invest in more pants, or I'll have to do the laundry more often."

"I don't have to kill people every day, no." Merihem was chuckling as he shook his head. "Gebre was a special case. Most of the time, the only fighting I do is when someone tries to get away, and that annoys me."

"That makes sense." Peni figured it wasn't anything he needed to see anyway, so he could worry about the laundry later. "How will we get to the forest? Is George all right, or is he still in hospital?"

"I'll translocate us." Merihem got up and started clearing their plates off the table. "George is out of hospital, but apparently, he's spending a bit of time in the forest as well. That's what Scott said, anyway."

"I'm glad he's all right." Peni sat and savored the moment, watching his mate clearing the table and stacking the dishes in the sink for Peni to take care of later. It was like a ritual for them now, and Peni loved that Merihem understood his love language so well.

"Ready to go?" Merihem held out his hand.

"Just don't be gone too long, or I'll worry," Peni said, although that was more for the demon than the human side. He could feel the warm glow of satisfaction coming from the demon as Merihem took them to the forest.

Half an hour later, Peni had forgotten about the dishes waiting for him back at the house. He was following Silas along a winding river, enjoying the scent of things growing, and the sound of the birds competing with the running water.

"You haven't been saying much." Silas nudged him gently with his shoulder. "Yet I sense you have a lot on your mind. Are things going all right with Merihem?"

"He's being wonderful." Peni sighed. "He would spoil me all day, every day if I let him. It's not the big things, you understand, it's more that he clears the dishes when we've finished eating, and he makes a point of wearing pants even in his demon form, and apparently, that's really unusual for him. He just gets me, I suppose." Clasping his hands in front of his chest, Peni smiled at his friend.

"And yet," Silas prompted.

"Have you met the Demon King, Asmodeus?" There was a rustle in the bushes back from the river, but Silas didn't seem worried about it, so Peni didn't worry either. It was probably Dakata trying to be invisible.

Silas shook his head. "No. Dakata has mentioned him a few times. It was Asmodeus who had an issue with Dakata in the demon realm after his rampage and punished Merihem for what happened during Wanda's rescue."

"I'm glad she's all right, too. That must've been really scary for her, being down there." Merihem had told Peni that story, and now he'd been to the demon realm, too, Peni could understand how brave Wanda had been.

"She's doing all right. We can't be separated from our trees for too long, and that was the biggest concern." Silas smiled. "But we care for our own around here, and we rescued her before anything major happened. Tell me about Asmodeus. What's he like?"

"He seemed really lonely." Peni struggled to put his thoughts in order. "He was super interested in the idea of mates and blissful ones, wanting to know what the difference was. I surprised him when I told him they were the same thing. He said about how Dakata and Merihem had both changed since claiming us..."

Silas's laughter made the leaves dance. "That's because we're special, and our demons put us first in everything. Most demons aren't like that. Dougal, the troll who has lived in this forest since the first trees started to grow, told me about that. That demons traditionally only care about themselves."

"See, I thought that, too." Peni nodded. "But Asmodeus was genuinely interested in what me and Merihem did together, and how Merihem behaved with me. He said there hadn't been a case of any demon finding their blissful ones for so long he truly believed they were a myth."

"And yet here we are." Silas's giggle bounced off the trees.

"Asmodeus is well aware of that." Peni had to giggle, too. "I was sitting in his private living room. You know, when I first saw him I thought I was going to pee my pants, but when he pulled Gebre into the throne room, and Merihem was going to fight him, Asmodeus just sat me on his arm. I felt like a parrot, I really did, and he told Merihem to come and find us when he was done. Behind closed doors, he's really different—kind and interesting."

"I guess that's why he's king."

"Well, that and he's as big as a house." It was nice, wandering along, chatting to a friend who Peni knew wouldn't judge him. "Asmodeus said he was passing on everything I've said to his scholars, people he has who record all the goings on in the demon realm. Apparently, you and I are really important. He even asked about our... you know, the stuff that goes on in the bedroom."

"Oh, my goodness. Were you all right about that?" Silas draped his arm over Peni's shoulder. "I know that's not something you're comfortable talking about."

"He was really nice about it. I guess he could see how embarrassed I was. My red cheeks don't lie." Peni pointed to his cheeks which were heating up. "But he was asking me about children and whether or not I ever wanted any."

"That's not something Dakata and I have talked about yet, either, but, oh, you should come and see. We already have children. My tree has three new sprouts that have shot up since Dakata and I got together."

Peni let Silas direct him back to the tree. "You call them your children, even though they're your trees. Do you call all the trees around here your children, too?"

"No. No, although they feel like family to me." Silas stroked a tree as they went past, and the leaves all rustled in his direction. "But my tree is an important part of my relationship with Dakata. You could say my demon and my tree have had *relations*."

"Mr. Dakata fucked your tree?" Peni slapped his hand over his mouth and shook his head. "I'm sorry. I didn't mean to say that. It just came out."

"It's fine." Silas was still smiling. "It's not like my demon stuck his dick in a tree knot or something, but the tree is part of me, and now it's part of us, and we have three new sprouts, which is wonderful as my tree has never sprouted offspring before."

Peni grabbed hold of Silas's arm and stopped him walking, even though he could see they weren't far from Silas's oak. "Is there... is it even possible for two males to have babies?" he whispered. "Only after Asmodeus asked about kiddies, and I did say I thought that would be a cute idea, but I had no idea how it could happen, he said that he did. I thought he meant, you know, the type of sex Merihem and I haven't had yet. But now..."

"Now?" Silas's eyes widened and then he did a head tilt thing, looking Peni up and down. "Have you taken Merihem's sperm into your body in any way?"

"That's what was so embarrassing when I met the king," Peni insisted. "We did the mouth thing, both of us, and I smelled like Merihem. Like I couldn't smell anything else. Do you think Asmodeus could smell it, too? Maybe that's why he did that weird thing."

"He's a demon, so I imagine he could smell it, but what weird thing did he do? Weirder than perching you on his arm like a parrot?"

Peni looked around, but his goat couldn't sense anyone else was around. "First, he sniffed me, and then... and then he blew on my face. And then in this really deep voice, he said, 'Your wish is my command,' like some person in a movie, but it wasn't a movie, it was me—he did that to me."

"How did you feel afterward? Did it make you sick? Did he have bad breath?"

Silas was teasing, but Peni remembered the moment as if it had just happened. "I know it seems like nothing, but there was magic in that breath, and I felt it go right through me. All over my body, right down to my toes. I didn't tell Merihem, and I felt all right afterward. But now... I've been getting a grumbly tummy in the mornings... I'm just being silly, aren't I?"

"I don't think you are." Silas tugged him over to the giant oak that towered high over the forest. Resting one hand on the bark and the other hand on Peni's shoulder, Silas's smile grew. "I knew it, and I think you know it, too."

"Know what?" All Peni could feel was tingles, which was probably the magic from the tree. Or maybe he needed something to eat.

"Congratulations. You're pregnant."

"I'm what!" Peni was sure his shout could be heard in the demon realm. It certainly scared the birds, who all disappeared in a flutter of wings.

Chapter Twenty-Three

Merihem

For the life of him, Merihem couldn't remember a time he'd been happier. He'd thought long and hard on this, but nothing seemed now to have given him the joy Peni did.

Was it sad that he got enjoyment out of washing dishes just to please his blissful one? Many would laugh their socks off at how the great Controller was now domesticated.

He shook his head, because he wouldn't be telling anyone how he behaved around Peni in their home. And it was their home, Peni had slowly added little personal touches around the house. This was the first reason for coming to the forest. Having left Peni with Silas, he stared at Dakata considering how best to ask for what he wanted.

"Spit it out," Dakata grumbled, his gaze focused on the direction of where Silas and Peni had disappeared.

"I want your house—to buy it."

Dakata's head whipped around to Merihem, and he wore a look that made Merihem chuckle.

"What? Didn't you think I'd want to live up here when this is where Peni is happiest?"

"You were always so adamant that the demon realm was your home, first and foremost."

Merihem shrugged and sighed. "Things change. You wouldn't go back, would you?" he asked, more out of interest.

"Never. Silas's soul is connected to his tree, as is mine now. But I'd already made the transition to this realm a long time ago. All I've done is move from one home to another. This is different for you."

Merihem eyed his friend. He wasn't wrong it was different, only it was in the best possible way, and he said so. "I didn't have a blissful one before. Being here with him is all I want. I don't want him in the demon realm for the same reasons as you. Silas's delicate disposition wouldn't cope, Peni is the same."

The nod came with a thoughtful look. "How will that work with Asmodeus? The king has had you as his right-hand demon for a long time."

For the first time in Merihem's long life, he was nervous. He'd heard nothing from the king, and he wasn't sure whether that was a good or a bad thing. "I don't know. I'm heading there next. That's why I brought Peni here for you to watch over him. And to ask about your house, which you haven't answered me," Merihem reminded him.

"The house, I'll gift to you both. You were there for me, my friend. Whatever you need, if it's within the realm of possibilities, it's yours."

The sincerity caused Merihem to take a moment to gather his emotions. His bond of friendship with Dakata was the most important of Merihem's life. He'd chosen well. He clasped Dakata to him and hugged him hard.

"Hey, what the fuck!" Dakata splutter-laughed before clapping him on the back. "You getting soft on me?"

"Fuck off," Merihem complained as he let go, grinning, not offended. "I've never been soft in my life." He flexed his arm, the T-shirt nearly tearing.

Dakata rolled his eyes. "Give over. You never impressed me, and at least one good thing came with Peni." His gaze dropped to his pants, and he waited for a beat. "At least I don't have to see your naked ass anymore."

"My blissful one doesn't like the idea of anyone seeing what belongs to him." Merihem was all smug satisfaction at that.

"Great... now, don't you think you should stop delaying and go and speak to Asmodeus?"

This was why they were friends, no bullshit, and he got what Merihem was doing—avoiding. "What if he refuses to let me continue as I am?" he asked, revealing his fear.

The serious expression that appeared as Dakata eyed him didn't help Merihem's cause. "Be honest. What can he do?"

"Say no!" Merihem and his demon side worried about that the most.

"Stop second-guessing what might happen and find out. Then we'll deal with it like we have always done."

They had. All of life's battles they'd fought together. Yes, Merihem had Peni now, but that was different. They strengthened each other with their bond, two parts of one whole perfectly matched. However, his friendship with Dakata was part of the foundation of Merihem's life. They used that platform to support each other and that would never change. "Thank you." Attached to those two words was the gravitas. "Keep Peni safe, I'll be back."

In a blink, he was in the demon realm outside the king's quarters, where he tended to be at this time of the day. Merihem took a deep breath and knocked on the door.

When it opened, Merihem found himself to be sweaty. He eyed the demon, who no longer wore the indulgent look he'd given to Peni.

"Ah, I see you have decided to give your king some of your precious time." The sarcastic bite to the words was like the tip of a whip slicing at skin.

Merihem didn't wince or show weakness, the king would use it against him. "Sorry for the delay."

A light flashed in Asmodeus' dark eyes before it disappeared, and Merihem had a chance to gauge what it was. "So it seems."

He swept back into the room, his robes trailing behind him as Merihem took that to be an invitation when the door hadn't slammed in his face. He shut it softly behind him, his mind racing on how best to lay out what he wanted. All his prepared speeches had somehow vacated his brain the second he'd seen the king.

Once the king sat on his throne wearing what could be classed as a bored expression, one that didn't fool Merihem, did he approach. "Sir..." he licked his drying lips, meeting Asmodeus' gaze head-on. "Sir, I have given consideration to my role within the demon realm—"

"When did it become your responsibility to consider what your role is in this realm?" The iciness dripped from the question.

Way to go to piss him off. His demon fought to break free. Seeing it might be for the best, Merihem receded. "We do not believe it is our responsibility, sir." The gruffness of his demon's voice was similar to the king's, only without the iciness. "But the last time we were here with Peni, I explained my blissful one would not be happy being in this realm. His happiness comes first, second, and everything in between."

The claw-like nails tapped on the arm of the throne, and Merihem's demon side was the one to sweat this time. Those dark eyes narrowed and pinned themselves on Merihem, holding him hostage. "Yes, I see you are telling the truth."

"Dakata has gifted me his home. Peni loves it there. It's his home now, and I want to live there permanently with him." Was he waffling? It felt like it!

You weren't doing any better. His demon side sounded miffed.

One brow arched giving him more of a demonic look and chilling Merihem's flesh. "That's kind of Dakata."

The way he said it wouldn't suggest that at all. "It was. I could, as I suggested, live in the human realm and carry out my role. Peni could stay with Dakata and Silas in the forest when I need to leave—"

"You are turning down my offer of Peni staying here with me? Do you think that I would not be able to protect your blissful one?"

The tone was flat and emotionless, however, his eyes held the fire of hell as they drilled into Merihem.

Oh, you're doing so much better than I was! Merihem couldn't stop himself from pointing it out. He fought to get back control from his demon half. The fucker wasn't playing ball.

He stood tall, even sitting on his throne, the king was slightly taller than Merihem's demon. "I have no doubt you could protect my blissful one. My problem is Peni would not be comfortable being here, sir. He is nervous and easily upset by things that he can't control in his environment. I do not wish to cause him any distress. Thinking and worrying about him would not be good for me in my position." All of what he said was the truth. And if that didn't work, then Merihem and his demon were going to have to resort to some other measure. What that might be...

He was clueless.

Time dragged as Asmodeus continued to hold his stare, Merihem didn't so much as flicker a muscle.

"Peni... did he speak with you about his visit with me?"

Huh?

The sudden change of conversation threw Merihem's demon for a loop. His lips parted and then closed. A sense of something came and went, but it was so quick that Merihem's human side didn't catch quite what it was. "He considered you were lonely."

What the fuck did you say that for? Merihem could only imagine that would piss the king off, and he braced.

When the king's lips twitched, Merihem gawked.

"He's sweet," he replied.

What was going on here? Had he fallen into a parallel realm?

"He is," they replied, for want of anything better to say.

"Did he mention anything else?" Asmodeus persisted, coming forward in his seat, looking almost excited.

"No. He just said that you had lots of questions, and he tried to answer them for you." The situation was getting more bizarre by the moment. "Erm, about leaving him with Dakata—"

The king waved his enormous hand, stopping him. "Yes, your blissful one can stay in the forest. Stress would not be a good thing in his condition. As you say, he's a sensitive soul and we wouldn't want to upset him. He'll have plenty to contend with in the future."

What the hell was he talking about?

"You must bring him for a visit again. I enjoyed my time with your little goat," he continued on.

"I'm sure he'd like that," Merihem muttered, frowning, still working on everything else the king had said. *Condition? What condition?*

"—You will need to check in with Badra on the list of deviants that require your attention. I assume Gebre won't have kept track due to his obsession with you, so you'll need to see him before you leave."

What had he missed? Merihem's demon nodded, but all Merihem could think about was the king's phrasing. *Condition. Plenty to contend with in the future?*

"You're dismissed. I'll let you know when I wish to see Peni again."

They were leaving and out of the throne room, the door shut behind them before Merihem knew what was going on. He felt he'd missed a chunk of what had gone on in the room.

What the hell was that all about?

I don't know what you're talking about.

The smugness of his demon side gave Merihem pause. *You're being a dick, you know that!*

I'm what! The words rang through Merihem's brain, making it rattle in his skull at the force of them. He didn't think as he translocated, any thoughts of visiting Badra gone at hearing his blissful one's distress.

Peni stood, pale as a ghost next to Silas who was smiling softly. Merihem's demon scanned the environment, heart pounding, claws at the ready as he put himself in front of Peni. Their senses found nothing. Nothing at all.

What is wrong, my love?

He scooped up Peni and kissed him on his clammy fore-head. "What happened?" he asked aloud when all he was getting was static from Peni. "Tell me, please."

Chapter Twenty-Four

Peni

"I want to squish your face in." Peni grabbed hold of the demon's face in both hands and squeezed with his fingers. It was akin to trying to squish a rock, but Peni was making a point. "I want to pound you, and squeeze you, and make your face all red. You… you…"

"My love, please. Tell me what's wrong."

"You don't know?" Peni wasn't sure he believed that. After hearing Silas's words and knowing what Asmodeus did, his brain was disjointed, and he just yelled the first thing that fell out of his mouth. "How can you not know? Demons know everything."

"Clearly not everything." Oh, look. Merihem's demon thought it would be funny to laugh. "I don't understand what's upsetting you. But if a mosquito bit you, I will hunt it down and annihilate it. If a blade of grass manages to tickle your ankle…"

"I've got socks on. Stop making fun of me."

Snuggle time. Snuggle time.

"It's not snuggle time, you silly goat." Peni patted his demon's face sharply. "As for you, pay attention."

"You have my absolute attention, my love."

"There you go again, spouting more nonsense. Listen. I'm a man, right? I have the same equipment as you?" Peni thrust his hips against Merihem's chest and then winced, because that was like pounding a rock as well.

"You have delightful bits." The hands on Peni's butt gave a little squeeze, but Peni couldn't get distracted when his brain had already splintered.

"You're making fun of me again. Do you remember…" Looking around, Peni saw Silas and Dakata were watching them. *What the heck? They'll all know soon enough anyway if they don't know already. The tree probably told them.* "When we did the mouth thing, a week ago. Do you remember that?"

"That first time you shared your body with me was one of the greatest memories of my very long existence."

"Good, then you'll remember that we both did the glug, glug, glug thing." Peni mimed a cock in his hand near his mouth while swallowing. "And I said about having a shower before we went to the demon realm, and you said no. Do you remember that?"

"Yes." Merihem's demon nodded, apparently getting with the program.

"And then I spent time with Asmodeus while you were doing your killing job."

Merihem's demon eyes flashed. "Did Asmodeus say or do anything to you?"

"He darn well did. He breathed on me!" Peni's voice rose as Dakata and Silas burst out laughing. Even the tree was waving around as if it was having fun, too.

"He breathed on you," Merihem repeated slowly, clearly doing his best not to join in the merriment, or so it seemed because Peni could feel he was holding back.

"You do not get to laugh at me." Peni tapped his demon's cheeks. "You do not get to laugh at *this*."

"I'm sorry." Merihem's demon swallowed hard, probably so he could hold the chuckles in. "So Asmodeus breathed on you. Did he sit too close? Did that frighten you? Could you smell the curry he had for lunch? I'm not sure... why are you bringing this up now?"

"You really don't know." Peni shook his head, ignoring his goat, who was sending him pictures of traipsing through the meadows in springtime with cute little kids in tow.

"I know something's distressing you, but I can't fix it if I don't know what it is."

"Well, you wanted to laugh. So laugh at this. I'm pregnant. Me. Pregnant." Once the words were out of his mouth, they took on a reality of their own. "I don't have lady bits. I'm fairly sure I don't have a womb. I've never even had a dick inside anything but my mouth. I've never done anything intimate with anyone except swallow for you, which I thought was perfectly normal and safe behavior, and clearly, it is unless you're mated to a demon.

"Because my demon wouldn't let me shower, I went to the demon realm smelling of sex and then a random Demon King, who I've only met the once blows right on my face, and now I'm carrying your baby, mate. A baby. *A bay-be.* That tree right there even told Silas it was true." He pointed at the giant oak, before resting his hands back on Merihem's face, and looking him straight in the eyes. "What do you have to say about that?"

There was no mistaking the wonder and affection in those fiery eyes. "You… I'm without words. You've given me the greatest honor. To know you're carrying our child…"

"Wait. Wait. Mister." Peni wasn't ready to give up his freak-out just yet. "Are you sure it's even yours? It was your king who breathed on me. And what type of baby would we have, anyway? Am I going to be carrying a little red demon goat? Or a baby with horns? Because if that's the case, then how in the demon realm is that baby meant to come out without ripping me apart?"

"The king has simply enhanced an act we did in love and has blessed us with something I never believed possible. It is our child. Yours and mine. Does it really matter what form it takes on arrival?"

"Well, when you put it like that…" *damn demon with his puppy dog eyes.* "It's not that I'm not happy about it, but you have to admit it's a tremendous shock to the system.

Wandering along the river one minute, complaining about a grumbly tummy to a friend, and then the next minute, bam! The congratulations start flying around."

"It's going to be all right." The hand that rested on Peni's face was hard, and yet so gentle. "The gift was not given to us as a means to tear us apart. Magic made this happen. Magic will assist the birth. Magic and the love we have for each other."

"I'll remind you of that when I'm the one yelling, *I can't see my feet*." Peni gave in then and snuggled into Merihem's neck. It seemed like the right thing to do. "Are you sure you're happy about it?"

"You have no idea, my precious love. I'm deliriously happy about it."

"Hey." Dakata came up, slapping Merihem on the back. "Congratulations, old man. I didn't think you had it in you. Come on into the house. Silas has got lunch for us. Might be a good idea to pull out a couple of wines or something to celebrate."

"No wine for me," Peni murmured. Merihem's demon's neck was so comfortable, and now his panic fit was over Peni was tired and hungry. "I'm pregnant."

Chapter Twenty- Five

Merihem

He continued to process that he was going to be a daddy days later as he finished banishing a demon, in several bits, from the realm. One he'd almost felt some sympathy for until the stupid ass decided to maim Merihem and got in a sly slice that he'd have to heal before he went to collect Peni. Merihem wasn't sure if his blissful one's hormones were catching. That was the second time he'd gotten caught out, something that had never happened before to him.

He released a sigh and wiped the blood down the leg of his sweats. The compromise he had gone for, when Peni was adamant about even doing his job in his realm, pants were a necessity. Merihem found a shop that had soft cotton sweats in his size and bought their entire stock. Killing could be a messy business when they got distracted.

I didn't get distracted. His demon half scoffed at that by making a rude noise.

Make sure you clean up properly, Merihem reminded his demon half.

You're worse than a hen fussing over her chicks.

There was no answer to that when Merihem did his best to never make Peni feel worked up. So he fussed. So what?

His demon side rolled his eyes, and then they were in the forest.

"What happened," Peni screeched. He was up and out of the seat where he'd been perched in the sunshine in a second.

See!

Merihem worked his magic, only Peni was faster. He grabbed at the arm where the long bleeding slice was. "Who did this to you?" he demanded. "Take us home. I need to take care of this. You could have all manner of germs in it. And you were just gonna flick your fingers or whatever without cleaning it!"

You did this on purpose! Merihem felt his demon's satisfaction at Peni's loving attention.

It was his turn to roll his eyes as they gave a wave to Silas who was sitting on Dakata's lap, both of them giving Peni indulgent glances before Merihem did as Peni requested.

At home, in their bedroom, his demon side receded. Peni dragged him into the bathroom, his little nose wrinkled as he eyed the bloody sweats. "Off, they need to come off. And you need a shower." He glanced at the shower stall, then back at Merihem, his brows tugging together. "I'm gonna have to come in with you."

Really!

Merihem nodded and flicked his fingers to save time getting rid of both their clothes. Peni was getting bolder at the touching, but as yet they'd not ventured beyond the bed when playing the skin-touching game. Since Peni had discovered he was pregnant, he definitely had enjoyed touching Merihem much more when naked.

When Peni looked at his naked body, his gaze remained on the part of him that was showing interest in what was happening. Merihem never pushed, but he did put out the occasional wish Peni would feel relaxed and try something new. Wet in the shower had lots of possibilities.

One more flick and the shower started drawing Peni's attention to the glass. "Washing… I'm washing you."

Merihem bit his lip at how his blissful one was more talking to himself—like it was a pep talk—than him. He let Peni guide him under the warm water and waited to see what came next.

The height difference made it impossible for Peni to kiss him, but he looked at Merihem's lips with intent as he took hold of his injured arm and washed it without once looking at it.

"Does it hurt?"

Merihem blinked the water out of his eyes and had to get his head in the game. "No." He was talking about his arm and not his dick. That hurt for sure with the hungry stare Peni was sizing him up with.

"Good." Little fingers ran over the cut delicately while his other hand held it under the spray. Yet still, Peni kept returning his focus elsewhere, making the ache in his balls increase. His cock stood fully erect, like a sword ready for battle.

Each gentle stroke was somehow connected to touching another part of him, and Merihem was back to biting his lip to hold back the moan and the urge to thrust his cock, knowing it would brush Peni's lower chest.

"I think I need to wash all of you... *just to make sure you're clean.*" Peni looked at the tiled floor. "You'll need to sit for me."

It was probably for the best because Merihem wasn't sure how much longer his legs could continue to hold him with how they shook. With a little manipulation, he sat on the hard, wet tiles, with Peni standing between his outstretched legs. Peni twisted around, presenting his delectable ass to Merihem as he grabbed the shower gel off the low shelf Merihem had fitted for him. Merihem shut his eyes, only he could recall vividly the ass flexing in his face as liquid trickled over his thighs.

Moments later, sparks set off an explosion inside him, a kaleidoscope of color formed in front of his eyes at the fingers working up his legs from his feet. He breathed in his blissful one's sweet scent, and his eyes opened and hooded at the sight of him.

The urge to lean in and taste made him shake as he resisted. Instead, he carefully stroked a fingertip down the swell of Peni's buttock.

The little ass tilted up a fraction. Was that an invitation? With his attention fully on Peni, he did it again, watching closely. Yes, it was a definite hip tilt towards him. The hands on his legs stopped moving as Merihem got a little bolder. He ran his fingertip down the crease of Peni's backside as his blissful one bent a little further forward. When Merihem reached Peni's hole, he swirled the pad of his finger over the rosebud.

Peni rested his hands fully on Merihem's thighs and groaned. His hole fluttered against his finger. Keeping the strokes slow and gentle, Merihem opened himself fully to Peni's emotions.

Wonder. Need. A little flustered at his own boldness. All were good, so Merihem continued to venture from his hole down his taint. He cupped his balls in his free hand and moved his finger out of the way of his questing tongue.

"N-no. Don't stop… ugh…" he cried just as the tip of Merihem's tongue touched his rosebud.

Sweetness and a flavor that was all Peni exploded over his tongue, and it was only the desire to please that kept him from devouring him.

Wow... a tongue... my ass... sensitive... more... gods... more.

Peni's thoughts, although scattered, Merihem got the drift. He cupped Peni's hips and lifted him onto his tongue when something came through loud and clear.

Deeper...

Pleaseeee...

Make it go deeper...

When he pushed the tip of his tongue, funneling it in slowly, then easing out before repeating the motion, Peni mewled and bucked into his face.

Taking direction from Peni, whether he was conscious of what he was doing, Merihem was ready to bust a nut. The second Peni's ass squished his tongue, the musky flavor filling his senses, Merihem's untouched cock exploded. He groaned and shuddered but never let go of his treat until Peni went lax in his arms. The scent of cum was strong in the shower's warmth.

He licked his lips as he rested Peni in his lap, cradling him to avoid the direct spray of water. He rested his head on Merihem's shoulder, peeking up at him shyly, melting his heart.

He kissed him, unable to resist. "Was that okay?" he murmured against his lips nervously.

Peni's cheeks flamed. "You have a very talented tongue." The cheeky grin he was giving Merihem made his spent cock twitch. "It's wasteful to not use such a talent, don't you think?"

Merihem's chuckles bounced off the glass in his delight. Nose to nose, he grinned. "Absolutely. And you know what they say about practicing?"

"What's that?" His smile matched Merihem's.

"Practice makes one perfect."

Giggles erupted from Peni. "Any more perfect and I might not get any cleaning done…" he glanced at the glass walls and sighed. "With all this glass, that would not be a good thing."

Back to chuckling, Merihem's smile was all teeth. "I'm sure we can find a replacement that won't get water spots on it." To keep that smile on his blissful one's face, Merihem would even clean it himself!

His demon was laughing his ass off.

Epilogue

Christa's
Obsession book
3 is a Sapphic
Romance

Wanda

"You're going to the city again? Why?" The words ran through Wanda's mind, the worry for her brother, it breathed within her. And it seemed for good reason. The conversations with Silas, her brother, gave her a strange sense of foreboding. Those senses never steered Wanda wrong. She always listened to them despite the fact that she couldn't often explain them if asked. Not that Silas asked, or would have listened to reason if she could tell him why she was concerned something bad was going to happen.

Silas believed in the good of people, and no one took her seriously.

She flounced off towards the river's edge, the evening breeze making her curls bounce around her cheeks.

Her green eyes glowed in the dying sun. It bathed her in an ethereal halo, surrounding her with its warmth. Her fingers ran over the blooms as she passed, offering what little she had left within her to the plants.

Dryads were supposedly solitary creatures, only bonding their spirit to a tree. Yet Wanda had never wanted to lose her connection with Silas. Their parents were long gone. Wanda, alone, had followed Silas to the forest where he had set down his roots, needing to keep her own rooted bond with him.

There she had come across an orchard. It sat on the far edges of the forest that Silas resided in, dying through neglect. The four peach trees left to fend for themselves, called to Wanda's soul. Silas having already bonded with his oak, his powers for healing could not be given to another tree, not in the way they needed to survive.

Wanda was unique because she had the ability to bond with all four trees without diminishing her gift. They would surely have perished if not for her willingness to share her magic.

By following Silas, she had expanded her family, something she secretly craved. Although she understood that no matter how hard she had tried to cling to Silas, as with all dryads, he was destined for something else.

She loved Silas very much only she didn't understand his need to leave the forest, but Wanda, the younger sibling, didn't crave anything beyond her orchard. Maybe a burger or two, whereas Silas wanted to head into the city and sing for those, who to Wanda's mind, didn't appreciate the pureness of his heart. She witnessed the destruction and carelessness of those who came into the forest. They left behind their garbage and trampled over the plants with no thought to the life they were hurting.

Dougal, Silas and Wanda helped maintain the balance of life in the forest and to Wanda, that was no greater gift.

So no, Wanda didn't want to leave the forest, her orchard, despite what Silas said about those he met. Sang for.

So here she was, fretting and terrified of all the changes that were happening in her small part of the world. Silas was a blissful one to a demon, no less. How this was possible, Wanda couldn't fathom.

Demons, weren't they evil creatures?

Destroyers of good?

Dougal, the troll of the forest, who was the font of all knowledge on such things as humans, shifter and all other beings, would have the answer, and all she had to do was ask. Only Wanda didn't know how to ask. To express her fear when Silas himself seemed—content—*excited* by this situation.

"You got somethin' on your mind, Wanda?" Dougal walked patiently at her side. As usual, he picked up her unease. The troll was perceptive.

She hesitated, then gave in, looking at Dougal as he walked quietly beside her like he had done a thousand times before. The troll wore a coat of many pockets, it never ceased to surprise her what he could find within it. "You're right I do."

She sighed, understanding talking to Silas about her worries wouldn't help when he saw things so differently to her. Her lips parted, then she stilled, listening out.

Head tilting, her curls tumbled around one shoulder at the voices that carried on the air. She didn't stop to think and took off, sensing where the interlopers were. "Someone's in my orchard."

The idiots were tramping around her trees.

"Slow down," Dougal called out after her.

"My trees need me," she called back, quickening her pace.

It wasn't the first time humans had come to take from the full branches of fruit. Wanda was happy to share, she just preferred they asked first. Her trees did not like anyone else touching them. They could get a little testy about such things.

"You there, what are you doing?" she called out when in sight of the two tall strangers. One of which was running his fingers down the bark of the smallest peach tree in a way that Wanda felt violated. Her tree shook the branches, trying to slap the hand away.

Stop them. Her trees demand had her running when the big brute didn't seem to notice he was getting whipped by branches.

The need to get them away overrode all common sense. "Stop that right now. They don't like to be touched by strangers. I don't go poking around your home touching your things, do I?"

They turned as one. An enormous wall of muscled chests, or so it seemed when they blocked the light, towering over her.

Eyes as dark as coal matched sneers that made everything inside Wanda scream for her to run. Their presence was unholy, yet the need to protect her family kept her right where she was. Chin poking out, doing her best to hide her fear.

The sense she was in serious trouble came too late when they grabbed hold of her arms, jerking her clear off the ground like she weighed nothing at all. She juddered violently at the feeling of their hands touching her skin. The dread she had felt earlier deepened. It attached itself to her heart, squeezing it in a painful, vice like grip.

Oh, to the forest goddesses!

She struggled to shake off the touch that sucked on the pureness of her soul.

"Great. The asshole got a dryad. That wasn't difficult." One of the men—demon grunted.

Wanda could sense the darkness surrounding his soul and her confusion at the words came with a slither of hope when she heard Dougal shout to let her go.

Only for violent shudders to run through Wanda, her stomach heaved and her eyes screwed shut when she felt herself leave the forest. The tight snap of the band severing from her trees cleaved her heart in two. The pain left her gasping for air.

"Get off me, you idiots," she gasped, hoping someone might hear and come to her rescue. "Put me down this instance." She kicked out her bare foot, and it was like kicking a tree. All it did was make her bare toes throb.

A hand smacked her cheek, the impact so brutal it made her head snap back and white spots dance in front of her wavering vision. Blood trickled out the corner of her mouth from where her teeth bit her lip. The throb of her toes didn't compete with the pain coming from her cheekbone, which she was positive that ham fisted ass had broken.

"Shut the fuck up," growled the one who hit her. They shook her violently, making her flap about like a shift on the breeze. A nauseating scent coming from them overshadowed the sweet smell of the peaches that lingered on her skin.

It was then that the air shimmered, and more demons appeared, all naked, they came closer, sniffing and pawing at her. "Let's hope Rainer says we can play with her."

A demon licked down her cheek to where her lip was bleeding and groaned sending terror through her soul.

Each breath dragged in the scent of blood, along with what she knew was death, degradation and sulfur. The darkness surrounding her broke with the cast of red lights, basking the room in a creepy glow.

Wanda whimpered, trying her best to stifle the need to cry out. Here she would know no pity when those beyond the walls in other rooms made inhuman sounds that sent panic through Wanda.

Flung down onto a chair that creaked and rocked at the force, the breath left her body. The room filled with yet more demons, larger, and scarier. Their cocks were hard and pushed closer to her face, arms, and chest. She shrank back, but to no avail.

Each touch painted her soul in misery. A sense of her life ending in this room came and Wanda could only pray it was a quick death. A death that Silas would thankfully not feel being in another realm.

"She's pretty enough, I suppose," a huge, naked red demon said, coming closer with ropes in his hand. His cock was enormous and engorged, brushing against her skin. "I bet I could make you look better, though, riding my cock. That would give you some color in those pale cheeks of yours." The menace stopped her blood pumping around her body.

She had no time to consider how to reply, a scream tore from her throat, "arggggggghhhh," at the large fist plowing into her unmarked cheek. The bone beneath shattering. She lost her vision when the pain hit her brain and registered as she slumped off the wooden seat. Only to find herself dragged back onto it as they used the rope to tie her to the chair.

Demon laughter rolled over her, much the same as the icky feel of the place, plucking at her sensitive skin, looking for ways inside.

More came into the room, her vision flickering with lights as Wanda tried to not let them feed off her pain and fear.

Tied to the chair, she much preferred the hitting rather than the turns they took, pawing at her, touching, taunting, and torturing her.

Endless pain, it sucked her to a husk. It came not only from their bodies, but from the separation of her trees. She had never left them since they had become a family, the broken connection left them exposed and her dying.

They would feel her pain, she could sense it.

She willed her death as her swollen eyelids drifted shut and sank into the pit of despair.

Sneak
Peek
Secretary's
Obsession
book 4

Scott

Brushing back his hair, Scott listened to Christa with half an ear, that was all he needed because he could easily keep up. His fingers flew over the iPad. He was taking notes for the concert that required organizing for the latest up-and-coming band. The music wasn't to Scott's taste, but he could understand the human appeal when the band was made up of good looking men in their early twenties.

"We need to speak to Vince and ask if we can have the venue for an additional night because the tickets sold out in three minutes, and the demand suggests it would be financially worthwhile."

Scott nodded, making an additional note to contact Vince. As a multitasker, Scott had learned long ago how to focus and prioritize what he needed to do first.

Dakata, a demon friend of his family, had built his music business from the ground up. When Scott had heard him complaining to his father about struggling to find someone in the human realm who was equipped to deal with Dakata's demands, Scott had offered to work for Dakata. Even though his family had scoffed at him, he excelled and had quickly become Dakata's right-hand demon.

Scott now knew the business inside out. Loved how he could slot all the pieces together to assist in making a band, or an event, reach its full potential.

"Are you listening to me?" Christa, Dakata's sister, questioned, one shapely brow arched to perfection while she swept her black flowing locks over one shoulder.

"Of course." Christa and her brothers did not focus on the details like Dakata, which was irritating, to say the least. Scott liked things organized and was not used to this current chaotic state the office was in.

But since Dakata had met his blissful one, which most demons, himself included, thought was more of a myth, things had changed. Scott had hardly recovered from the shock when Merihem, Dakata's best friend—who had become forced by the Demon King to come and work for Dakata because of a minor issue in the demon realm—had found his blissful one, too.

It was as if it was catching...

"Are you going to go? It seems rather urgent?" Christa's voice penetrated past his thoughts, and he kept his expression totally neutral at being caught—for the first time—not paying attention.

He stared at Christa, hoping to gauge what he'd missed. When he got nothing, he ignored the smug smile at not being able to read her and swallowed his sigh of frustration.

"Merihem reached out. He's been in an accident—"

"What!" Up off the seat, his concern for Merihem, who he genuinely liked, his sleeping demon stirred for the first time that day. His demon side hated office work, so much so that he spent most of the day sleeping when Scott was at work.

"He's fine, as is Peni. They need you to go to them because of the cab driver, George, he needs to go to the hospital," Christa explained as she wrote on a piece of paper.

A moment later, she pushed it over the table towards him, and he picked it up, seeing an address for a street he didn't believe was that far away. He gave her a searching look, his concern for those he knew now held in check.

He didn't jump to conclusions. "This cab driver, why is he important?"

Christa's expression grew grave, and Scott's demon paid attention. "He is a friend of Silas's and injured seriously enough that he isn't able to shift to heal that's unusual. Merihem wants to ensure he's looked after. Can you do that?"

"Of course."

"Get him whatever he needs," Christa added, like Scott needed the added instructions, when he didn't.

Scott used his iPad to search for the details of the nearest hospital to where the accident was, working out the logistics. He often chose not to translocate, he much preferred human travel. It was less taxing when his demon wasn't always awake.

The movement of Christa sitting back in her seat, crossing a silk-clad leg over the other, got Scott meeting her gaze. A light of amusement was there in the depth of her eyes. "Are you going? He's unconscious and has no one to advocate for him." She pointed at his tablet. "What are you doing?"

"He may possibly have healed before I get there. But I'm looking at the hospitals in the area, assessing likely courses of action for the paramedics." Shifters, like demons, had the ability to heal themselves. The bear would probably be gone before Scott got there. Clearly, it was going to be a waste of his time.

He expressed none of his thoughts on the matter, while he considered what he would have to shuffle around to make sure he met all the personal deadlines he set himself to keep everything in order.

Christa gave him a seductive smile, one that would never work on Scott, as he wasn't interested in females or dating another demon. They were all arrogant, and he'd had enough of that to last him a lifetime with his family. He liked calm and orderly, not chaotic or rampaging. It just wasn't him.

"Possibly, but our guys are worried about the bear, so just check on them and him. I'll sort through what's needed here, so don't worry." She clearly got what his reluctance was. Christa or her brothers had no talent for organization, to Scott's mind.

He nodded, spun around on his Italian loafers, and left the room, keeping the worry about how she'd achieve the things on the long list he'd established to keep her on track. When Christa went off in the opposite direction from Scott's way of working, it was troublesome. But he got paid handsomely, so he didn't complain.

At his desk, he tidied everything away in its place and tucked the iPad in his laptop bag. He would work at the hospital while they did whatever was needed so as not to waste time.

Scott released a quiet sigh at thoughts of this disruption and messaged Dakata's driver.

With his laptop bag slung over his broad shoulder, two minutes later he slipped out of the building. Dakata's car and driver were waiting for him. He moved swiftly and got into the back seat, the scent of leather greeting his nose. He settled back and immediately pulled out his laptop, resting it on his knees before giving the street address to the driver.

Minutes passed, and Scott lost track of time as he sent emails and re-organized his workload. When he glanced up as the car slid to a stop next to a police car, he looked at the scene of carnage. His pulse leaped at the mangled car.

Seeing Merihem holding a small goat, Scott tucked his laptop away and got out of the car, striding past the wreckage, and considered that Merihem and Peni were lucky to escape.

Seeing a glimpse of a person on a trolley inside as he passed the ambulance, he noted the doors shutting before he reached Merihem.

He'd barely come to a stop when Merihem demanded, "Scott, give this officer details of where to find me." There was no waiting for a reply, Merihem stalked off with his blissful one in his arms.

Scott offered a polite smile, pulling out a card from his wallet. "You can contact this number, and I will organize a suitable time to discuss the accident."

Scott didn't acknowledge the blustering officer, he just repeated himself once more before leaving to go back to the car when the ambulance sirens blared as it drove off.

There were several bleats coming from Peni when Scott got into the back of the car. Seated, he glanced at Merihem. "Where to?" Scott tugged on the cuff of his suit jacket, crossing his legs.

"Take us to Dakata's house."

Scott gave the instructions to the driver, while he listened to Merihem work to coax Peni to shift into his human form.

Scott watched in fascination when a rather giddy goat attempted to climb Merihem's chest.

When they came to a stop, Merihem looked flushed, and his efforts to get Peni to shift had been unsuccessful.

"I need you to follow up with George, the cab driver. Go to the hospital and pay any bills for his care. See that they look after him."

Scott nodded, knowing already that would be his next task. "Of course."

Merihem got out of the car, buck naked. Scott heard a woman walking past gasp. Peni bleated and kicked his hooves in the woman's direction when she stopped to stare.

Scott held back a chuckle when he heard Merihem whisper, "that told her," which earned him a lick to his face from the goat.

When Merihem returned his attention to the open door and Scott, he grinned. "I'll not be in the office for the rest of the week. Can you email me everything you want me to look at and courier over anything requiring signing?"

"Of course."

Back with his laptop on his knee, Scott pulled up a schematic of the emergency department while tracking the ambulance via the street cameras. Not strictly legal, but it allowed him to know exactly where George was and would end up.

When they stopped some time later behind the same ambulance, Scott closed down his laptop and set it aside. "Please find somewhere to wait, I'll call you when I'm ready to leave."

"Yes, sir."

Out of the car, Scott strode into the emergency room, his nose twitched at the scents assaulting him. He went to the desk where people stood queuing. He patiently waited his turn.

The woman behind the counter didn't even bother to look at him as he stepped forward. "How can I help you?" she asked in a bored tone.

"I'm looking for George Maybank. He was brought in after an accident involving several people."

"Are you a relative?" She tapped at the keyboard.

"Yes," he lied, not wanting to explain why he was there or who had sent him.

Gum moved its way around her teeth as she blew a bubble, and it popped as she finally glanced up at him. When she got a look at him, the bored look disappeared. A smile appeared, he supposed she thought was flirty.

His blond good looks and dimples often got this reaction. "He's in the emergency bay for assessment and observation."

"Thank you." He spun about and walked off, not needing anything more.

"Sir, you can't go back there," she called after him.

He merely nodded to confirm he'd heard her and continued on. He glanced about looking for a place to translocate, unobserved into the emergency department.

He followed the signs and stepped into a side ward, then gave himself a moment to think about what he'd seen on the schematic before he translocated. No one noticed his arrival. How would they when it looked like a demon had been through the area on a rampage?

People moved hastily, darting past obstacles as they went about their business. Twice he tried to attract someone's attention and then gave up.

He walked to the electronic board that displayed patients' names and locations. He noted the one he needed and easily found the cubicle.

Scott glanced about, listening when he came to a stop at a half-drawn curtain around a gurney with a large pair of booted feet hanging off the end.

Scott's demon chose then to wake up fully. *Why are we in a smelly hospital? And who is that little honey?*

Little honey? To whom are you referring?

His demon side chuckled at him. *You need to remove that stick from your ass occasionally.*

Behave.

Hey, I'm just saying it how it is. And who is the honey bear?

Scott glanced at the gurney, not quite seeing a honey bear, but then his demon could be whimsical occasionally. *He's a friend of Silas.*

The enormous man smelled like a bear, but there was no sweet honey smell. Dark, wavy brown hair hung around a rugged face. A wound to the left side of his head showed why he was there. The black and purple bruising didn't detract from how handsome he was.

Handsome.

Maybe he'd taken a hit to the head! Or maybe his demon was pushing the thought into his head?

He's sexy, his demon purred, and Scott rolled his eyes heavenward.

You think any guy with legs is sexy. It was the truth.

The chuckling continued in his mind and made Scott reluctant to see what his demon would do when he got closer. But he had a duty to check on the bear, and that's' what he would do.

Stepping behind the curtain, Scott caught a flicker of eyelid movement from the bear. His body froze and something flowed through him, an awareness that made him hyper-alert and attuned to his demon. Something that so rarely happened he braced—for what he couldn't say—as he watched those eyes move with a sense of dread.

When they fluttered open, Scott forced his lips into a smile to give reassurance because he didn't need the bear freaking out on him. Only the moment their eyes connected, Scott's demon, who was not one to be a nuisance or cause trouble, wanted out. He surged so hard that if not for the gurney in front of him, he'd have been forcibly thrown to the ground. Instead, Scott had to reach out and grab the rail to stay upright.

He panted, his insides spiraling out of control at the need from his demon side to touch the bear. His hands clawed as he struggled to hold back.

What on earth is wrong with you?

Ours!

About the
Author

Lisa Oliver lives in the wilds of New Zealand, although her beautiful dogs Hades and Zeus are now living somewhere else far more remote than she is. Reports indicate they truly enjoy chasing possums although they still can't catch them. In the meantime, Lisa is living a lot closer to all her adult kids and grandchildren which means she gets a lot more visitors. However, it doesn't look like she's ever going to stop writing - with over a hundred paranormal

MM (and MMM) titles to her name so far, she shows no signs of slowing down.

When Lisa is not writing, she is usually reading with a cup of tea always at hand. Her grown children and grandchildren sometimes try and pry her away from the computer and have found that the best way to do it is to promise her chocolate. Lisa will do anything for chocolate… and occasionally crackers. She has also started working out, because of the chocolate and the crackers.

Lisa loves to hear from her readers and other writers (I really do, lol). You can catch up with her on any of the social media links below.

I finally got my Patreon page up and running – you can check that out at

Facebook –

Official Author page –

My new private teaser group -

My MeWe Group -

And Instagram -

My blog -

Twitter – _

Email me directly at yoursintuitively@gmail.com.

Other Books By Lisa Oliver

Please note, I have now marked the books that contain mpreg and MMM for those of you who don't like to read those type of stories, or for those who prefer them Hope that helps ☺

Cloverleah Pack

Book 1 – The Reluctant Wolf – Kane and Shawn

Book 2 – The Runaway Cat – Griff and Diablo

Book 3 – When No Doesn't Cut It – Damien and Scott

Book 3.5 – Never Go Back – Scott and Damien's Trip and a free story about Malacai and Elijah

Book 4 – Calming the Enforcer – Troy and Anton

Book 5 – Getting Close to the Omega – Dean and Matthew

Book 6 – Fae for All – Jax, Aelfric and Fafnir (M/M/M)

Book 7 – Watching Out for Fangs –Josh and Vadim

Book 8 – Tangling with Bears – Tobias, Luke, and Kurt (M/M/M)

Book 9 – Angel in Black Leather – Adair and Vassago

Book 9.5 – Scenes from Cloverleah – four short stories featuring the men we've come to love

Book 10 – On the Brink – Teilo, Raff and Nereus (M/M/M)

Book 11 – Don't Tempt Fate – Marius and Cathair

Book 12 – My Treasure to Keep – Thomas and Ivan

Book 13 – Home is Where the Heart is – Wesley and Castor

The Gods Made Me Do It (Cloverleah spin off series)

Book One - Get Over It – Madison and Sebastian's story

Book Two - You've Got to be Kidding – Poseidon and Claude (mpreg)

Book Three – Don't Fight It – Lasse and Jason

Book Four – Riding the Storm – Thor and Orin (mpreg elements [Jason from previous book gives birth in this one])

Book Five – I Can See You – Artemas and Silvanus (mpreg elements – Thor gives birth in this one)

Book Six – Someone to Hold Me – Hades and Ali (mpreg elements but no birth)

Book Seven – You'll Know in Your Heart – Baby and Owen (mpreg)

Book Eight – Worth It – Zeus and Paulie (mpreg)

Book Nine – When Three Points Collide – Ra, Kirill and Arvyn (M/M/M) (mpreg elements, no birth)

Book Ten – Special Enough – Odin and Evan

Book Eleven – Reconciliation: Seth's Story – Seth and Luka (mpreg is a small part of this story)

Book Twelve – Being Loki - Loki and Anubis

Book Thirteen – Give Me A Reason – Helios and Bruno

Book Fourteen – Fenrir's Fate – Fenrir and Dorian

Book Fifteen – Wanting to Belong – Hephaestus and Landyn

The Necromancer's Smile (This is a trilogy series under the name The Necromancer's Smile where the main couple, Dakar and Sy are the focus of all three books – these cannot be read as standalone).

Book One – Dakar and Sy – The Meeting

Book Two – Dakar and Sy – Family affairs

Book Three – Dakar and Sy – Taking Care of Business

Bound and Bonded Series

Book One – Don't Touch – Levi and Steel

Book Two – Topping the Dom – Pearson and Dante

Book Three – Total Submission – Kyle and Teric

Book Four – Fighting Fangs – Ace and Devin

Book Five – No Mate of Mine – Roger and Cam

Book Six – Undesirable Mate – Phillip and Kellen

Stockton Wolves Series

Book One – Get off My Case – Shane and Dimitri

Book Two – Copping a Lot of Sin – Ben, Sin and Gabriel (M/M/M)

Book Three – Mace's Awakening – Mace and Roan

Book Four – Don't Bite – Trent and Alexi

Book Five – Tell Me the Truth – Captain Reynolds and Nico (mpreg)

Alpha and Omega Series

Book One – The Biker's Omega – Marly and Trent

Book Two – Dance Around the Cop – Zander and Terry

Book Three – Change of Plans - Q and Sully

Book Four – The Artist and His Alpha – Caden and Sean

Book Five – Harder in Heels – Ronan and Asaph

Book Six – A Touch of Spring – Bronson and Harley

Book Seven – If You Can't Stand the Heat – Wyatt and Stone (Previously published in an anthology)

Book Eight – Fagin's Folly – Fagin and Cooper

Book Nine – The Cub and His Alphas – Daniel, Zeke and Ty (MMM)

Book Ten – The One Thing Money Can't Buy – Cari and Quaid

Book Eleven – Precious Perfection – Devyn and Rex

Book Twelve – More Than a Handful - Karl and Tanner

Spin off from The Biker's Omega – BBQ, Bikes, and Bears – Clive and Roy

Balance – Angels and Demons

The Viper's Heart – Raziel and Botis

Passion Punched King – Anael and Zagan

Soul Deep – Uriel and Haures

Found – Raphael and Seir

Demon Masks and Angel Wings – Michael and Orobas

Love Before Time – Lucifer and Gabriel

Arrowtown

A Tiger's Tale – Ra and Seth (mpreg)

Snake Snack – Simon and Darwin (mpreg)

Liam's Lament – Liam Beau and Trent (MMM) (Mpreg)

Doc's Deputy – Deputy Joe and Doc (Mpreg)

Cam's Chance – Cam and Fergus (Mpreg)

Stone Cold Obsidian – Dian and Kee (Mpreg)

Brutus's Surprise – Brutus and Heath

Hal's Silence – Hal and Blade (mpreg although not the main focus of the story)

City Dragons

Dragon's Heat – Dirk and Jon

Dragon's Fire – Samuel and Raoul

Dragon's Tears – Byron and Ivak

The Magic Users of Greenford – a new trilogy.

Book One - Illuminate

Book Two – Eradicate

Book Three – Validate

Words Not Necessary – Rocky and Neo – a spin off short story from this world.

My Arranged Marriage Fantasy Romance Books (not Fated Mates)

The Infidelity Clause – Nikolas and Caspian

Don't Judge A Prince by his Undergarments – Mintyn and Syrius

An Article of Lies – Xavier and Remy

The Pirate's Treasure – Rojan and Petrov

A Marriage of Necessity – Jasper and Avalon

Six Types of Apology – Vincent and Orion

Quirk of Fate

Summons – Edward and Mammon

Reggie's Reasons – Reggie and Dirkin

The Mating of Blind Billy Hipp – Billy and Dathan

Demon Dabbling – Zese and Percy

Quirk of Fates Shorts

Saving Moses – Tucker and Moses

Catching Damont – Damont and Rebel

Not A Typical Meet Cute – Locryn and Zac

Hellhound Collar Series

Collar and Scruff (Prequel) – Raoul and Jason

Better Than Sweets (Book 1) – Java and Cyril

Precious Blue (Book 2) – Beau and Blue (mpreg elements in last chapter.)

Cain's Shadow – Cain and Ollie (mpreg)

Cooking With Magic – Faron and Patrick

Assassin's Alley

Not that Kind of Demon – Python and Cyrus

Sweet Things for a Crocodile – Storm and Pax

Benedict and Bear Trilogy

Benedict and Bear #1 – Benedict and Dixon

Benedict and Bear #2 – What's Done is Done

Tangled Tentacles – in Collaboration with JP Sayle

Book one – Alexi – Alexi and Danik

Book 2 – Victor – Azim and Victor (mpreg)

Book 3 – Todd – Todd, Lucas, and Ki – MMM (mpreg)

Book 4 – Markov – Markov and Cassius

Book 5 – Kelvin – Kelvin and Magnus (mpreg - Markov)

Assassins To Order With JP Sayle

Marvin – Marvin and Ajani

Ben – Ben, Nico, and Teilo (MMM)

The Baby Question – a short story catching up with men from the Tangled Tentacles and Assassin series (MM, MMM and Mpreg)

Duron – Duron and Beaumont

Conrad – Conrad and Kylo (mpreg elements)

Dancing With The Devil – Wyatt and James (mpreg)

Standalone:

I Should've Stayed Home: Irwin's Story – Part of the Nocturne Bay collab series – Irwin and Kolton

The Fall of the Fairy Tale Prince – Charlie and Lex (A spin off from Dancing Around the Cop and Change of Plans in the A&O series)

Stay True to Me – Con and Ven

Rowan and the Wolf – Rowan and Shadow

Bound by Blood – Max and Lyle – (a spin off from Cloverleah Pack #7)

The Power of the Bite – Dax and Zane

One Wrong Step – Robert and Syron

Uncaged – Carlin and Lucas (Shifter's Uprising in conjunction with Thomas Oliver)

Also under the penname Lee Oliver/Lisa Oliver

Northern States Pack Series

Book One – Ranger's End Game – Ranger and Aiden

Book Two – Cam's Promise – Cam and Levi

Book Three – Under Sean's Protection – Sean and Kyle

Book Four – Newton's Law – Newton and Tron

Oher
Books by
JP Sayle

Standalone

When Fake Changed Everything

Christmas beyond Christmas

The Elves and the Bondage Daddy (Grim and Sinister Delights Book 5)

Agrippa My Heart

His Boy to Tease

Headshot

A Brat For Kinkmas

Hanging With Daddy

A Little Christmas Matty Secret

A Little Christmas Terrence

A Sucker For Christmas

Music & Dreams

Magic Demon & the Hunter

Cruising Right Into Love

Series

Assassins To Order With Lisa Oliver

Marvin – Marvin and Ajani

Ben – Ben, Teilo & Nico

Duron – Duron & Beaumont

Conrad – Conrad & Kylo

Dancing With the Devil – Wyatt & James

Tangled Tentacles Series with Lisa Oliver

Alexi #1

Victor #2

Todd #3

Markov # 4

Kelvin # 5

Little Paws Haven Series

Little Treasure he Hides JP Sayle & Lisa Oliver

Little & Lethal JP Sayle & Layla Dorine

Weird & Wacky Shifters

All He Wants For Christmas is a Fingerling

Alpha's Fingerling Surprise

A Boy Called Blu

The Potters Creek Series

A Christmas Wish (book one)

The App Series

The App: Daddy kink (book one)

The App: Littles (book two)

The App: Puppy play (book three)

The Flamingo Bar Series

Always More (book one)

The Little Side of Me (book two)

3 Is the Magic Number (book three)

La Trattoria Di Amore Series

Puzzle Pieces (book one)

Dominated but not Subdued (book two)

Made to Submit

The Playroom Series

Mine, Body and Soul: Part One

Mine, Body and Soul: Part Two

Mine, Body and Soul: Part Three

Ferron's Journey: Damaged Part One (book four)

Ferron's Journey: Hidden Part Two (book five)

Ferron's Journey: Revelation Part Three (book six)

Mine, Body and Soul Trilogy

Ferron's Journey Trilogy

Spinoff Love's Heart Print

Dark River Stone Collective Series

The Light Beneath the Dark (Book One)

When Darkness Turns to Light (Book Two)

Running From Darkness (Book Three)

The Billionaire Playground Series

Property of a Billionaire (Book one)

Reluctant Billionaire (Book two)

Billionaire's Muse (Book three)

Heart Stones Series

Blood King

The Manx Cat Guardians Series Where it all Began: Origins (Book 1)
Seeing Beyond the Scars (Book 2)
Destiny Collides Past and Present (Book 3)
Searching for a Soul to Love (Book 4)
The 12 Disasters of Christmas (Book 5)
Laws of Attraction (Book 6)

The Teacher's Boy (Book 7)

Boxset

Audio Books

Mine, Body and Soul, Part One: The Playroom Series

Mine, Body and Soul, Part Two: The Playroom Series

Mine, Body and Soul, Part Three: The Playroom Series

Daddy Kink: The App (book one)

Always More: The Flamingo Bar (book one)

When Fake Changed Everything

Ferron's Journey: Damaged Part One

Ferron's Journey: Hidden Part Two

Ferron's Journey: Revelation Part Three

Romance books in a mixed series of M/F and M/M by the Author under a different pen name Jayne Paton

Smith's Corner

Delilah & Dallas (book one)

Layla & Levi (Book two)

Ash & Alora (Book three)

Fox & Faith (book four)

Storm & Stone (book five)

Hunter & Holden (book six)

Crime and Thrillers by the Author under a different pen name J Paton

Headspace

Chozen: Dark MM Crime Drama (Headspace Book 1)

Chozen: Dark MM Crime Drama (Headspace Book 2)

About the Author JP Sayle

Eccentric cake lover who has a passion for words of all kinds. I'm Jayne or JP, I live in the Isle of Man. A tiny place in the Irish sea where all the magic happens. I'm a confessed bookaholic and if I'm not writing I love to snuggle with a book or two…if you catch my drift.

If you're interested in keeping up to date, then I've a few places you can do that, and they're listed below. My website is where you'll find all the different Me's there are, LOL. As I travel this path into the future, I'm going to be writing in different genres so to stop there being any confusion I'll be writing under different pen names.

If you would like to give me any feedback or just have any questions, go ahead and friend me on Facebook, and I would be happy to answer anything. I hope you enjoyed this book and if you would also like to leave a review, then I would love to read your thoughts. Even if you just want to rate it, I'll be grateful

Thank you for being a part of my dream.

Newsletter Sign up

Goodreads

Tumblr

Bookbub

Instagram

Twitter

Facebook

Website address

Facebook Author page

JP Manx Minx's

Patreon